**FRIENDS
OF ACPL**

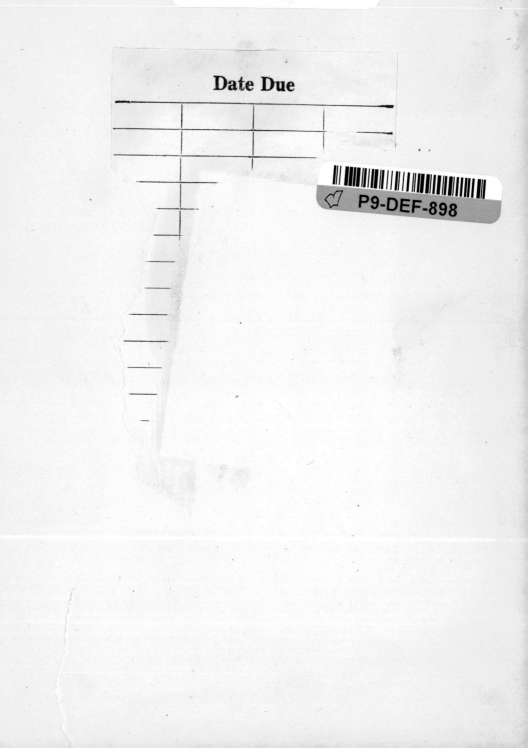

Date Due

ALICE-ALL-BY-HERSELF

Alice-All-by-Herself

BY

ELIZABETH COATSWORTH

Pictures by

MARGUERITE DE ANGELI

New York

THE MACMILLAN COMPANY

1946

To Maurice and Beatrice Day

who are Alice's godparents

CONTENTS

CONTENTS

ILLUSTRATIONS

ALICE-ALL-BY-HERSELF

Alice, if you'll forgive an acrostic,
Let me present my heart's bouquet,
I love the Northland, its tales and its people,
Country and village, headland and bay—
Eyes clear as yours are a mirror, they say.

I

AS IN DAYS OF OLD

THE big square white house where Alice lived had been built by the ancestor who was a ship captain, but the kitchen ell was much older. It had been part of the original house built in the middle of the eighteenth century on land bought from the Indians. Alice had seen the deed signed by her great-great-great-grandfather and the chief whose mark was a running deer. Her father had some of the old letters, too, telling of how the first of the family to settle in Maine had skirted the coast in his little shallop and liked the location on the Damariscotty River, as he spelled it then, near the old colonies of Pemaquid and the Sheepscot.

He had paid a fair price for his land and after that a sort of yearly rent in cornmeal, and he had really liked the Indians. More than once he gave them advice in their affairs with the whites and on several occasions they had given him warning of intended incursions of the French and Indians from around Quebec. His young bride wrote back to Boston that when she came down in the morning she never knew how many Indians she might find in the kitchen wrapped in their blankets, asleep, with their feet to the fire. In time she grew used to it. They never stole anything and in return for their shelter they sometimes brought her berries and venison. The old, rather brittle basket in which the eggs were still kept had been given to this ancestor by one of the squaws, filled with wild strawberries, and the clothespins were still kept in a square box of birch bark with designs of lighter and darker layers, whose top had long ago been broken.

Alice often thought about Indians, but she had never seen one until the day her father brought back Raymond in the rumble seat of the Ford. He had seen the boy walking along the road with his bundle neatly wrapped in newspaper, and picked him up. There were many men looking for work that summer, and Alice's father always did what he could to help them.

2

Alice and her mother were weeding the bed of flowers near the door when her father came home with the quiet, thin, rather awkward-looking young man with a boyish face and dust-colored hair.

Alice's father sent him in to Olga for something to eat and then came over to her mother.

"He seems a very nice lad," he told her. "In spite of his hair, he's a Passamaquoddy Indian and can't read or write. I thought that if Olga would fix up the shed chamber, he could stay here for a few weeks and do some of the odd jobs that need to be done—that is, if you would like it."

Alice waited eagerly for her mother's answer.

"It sounds like a very good idea," said Alice's mother, after thinking a moment. "I have nothing that has to be done— Alice and I will fix up a place for him right away."

Alice, thrilled at the idea of an Indian in the house again, carried the broom and dustpan and brush, and her mother brought sheets and blankets. The shed chamber was only a kind of attic over the shed with windows at one end and cracks in the floor. In the shadows one could see boxes and the dark mouth of an old Franklin stove and the circle of a spinning wheel, but by the light there was a bed, with its mattress rolled at its foot. When Alice and her mother had finished, the shed chamber looked quite gay, with turkey-red curtains at the window, the bed covered with a log-cabin patchwork

3

quilt, a rag rug on the floor beside the bed, and fresh water in the pitcher on the stand.

Raymond was a very good worker and he had a natural courtesy. Since he never read, he watched everything. He always seemed to know what a person wanted before the person really knew it himself, and would hand Alice's father a tool or bring Olga a dish which they were just beginning to realize that they needed. All the wisdom of his people he knew in hundreds of handy sayings—that the bow paddle of a canoe should come to the chin and the stern paddle to a man's brow, that the bottom of a sink should be level with one's wrists, that a new baby should be put in new things: he had an appropriate opinion for every common occurrence of daily life.

In two days he was thoroughly part of the household. It seemed as though he had always been there, trimming dead wood in the orchard, draining the wet place in the meadow, bringing in Bessie's milk in the morning and late afternoon. But Alice never lost her sense of excitement at knowing that he was an Indian.

One day a cousin of her mother's was visiting them and asked to be taken to the famous shell heaps on the river.

"May I go, too, father?" asked Alice. "I've never been there."

"What, haven't you?" asked her father, surprised. "But

it's always that way. We'll go thousands of miles to see some wonder, but never the one that's just across the street. Now's your chance, Alice. Mother and I have to stay home to see someone this afternoon, but Raymond will drive Cousin Martha and you over to the shell heaps and I'll tell you just where to go."

A mile out of town they stopped the car by the roadside and followed a lane between two barns, and down toward the river that gleamed below them. Twice Raymond took down the bars of a gate for them to cross through, and there was a thicket of wild apples on one side, and in the hollow behind the shell heaps there was the remnant of a round cellar and bricks where once a pioneer's cabin may have stood, near the river which was then their only road. When they had scrambled down to the beach, they could see that the steep hillocks were composed entirely of oyster shells, some broken and some still whole, but very old and brittle: opposite them across the smooth rush of the incoming tide were heaps perhaps forty feet high, crowned with trees, rising up sheer from the water's edge, and dazzlingly white above the dark river.

"Father says there aren't any oysters here anymore," said Alice. "He says it must have taken hundreds of years, maybe thousands, to make these heaps."

All three of them sat down on stones and were rather quiet

5

after that. The afternoon sunlight was very warm and golden; it threw long shadows of pines across the smooth upward flow of the river. Near them the two currents, the fresh water going down the river and the salt water forcing its way up, met in a series of sharp, singing ridges, and here for a moment appeared the round, sleek head of a seal before it gave a sort of slow cartwheel and disappeared.

Here and across on the opposite bank the neighboring tribes must have gathered every summer for their feasts. With wandering people like the Indians, whose graves and village sites faded back into the wilderness in a few years, these shell heaps must have seemed like monuments to their own long existence and their merriment.

Raymond looked at them rather sadly. "If all the Passamaquoddy Indians and all the Old Town Indians ate all the clams they could eat for a week, it wouldn't be as big as *that*," and he pointed to a boulder. Then he added, "All the oysters are gone and most of the Indians," and lighted a cigarette.

There seemed nothing more to say. But Alice was in a daydream again. She was an Indian girl in a doeskin dress, and she was coming down the river in a white birch canoe with two stars of colored porcupine quills at the bows. Her Indian father and mother were in the canoe, and a small fat papoose who never cried. As they came near the shell heaps,

6

they saw all their friends encamped under the trees and they shouted at them. . . .

"I suppose we must be going back," said Cousin Martha. "Your mother spoke about tea."

Cousin Martha and Alice each picked up a few shells to take with them, crumbling shells that had once been dripping and full and bearded with weeds.

"I wish I could find an arrowhead," said Alice.

Raymond began to scan the ground, and then he shook his head. "After a rain," he said, "then the flint shows up shinier than the other stones."

But for once a special luck showed Alice's dreaming eyes something which Raymond's keener look missed.

As they scrambled up the steep bank of the shell heap holding on to roots and small bushes that lined the path, Alice saw to one side a woodchuck's burrow, with a flat platform of broken shells and earth in front of it, which seemed to have been recently dug out. Something drew Alice over toward the hole; these little dark houses in the earth with their verandahs of materials so long buried away from the sun, always seemed mysterious to her. Today she had every reason to think so, for lying in full sight by the door of the burrow was an arrowhead, no more than an inch long, of purest white quartz, almost transparent, its edges as clear-cut and lovely as though they had only been chipped out the

7

day before. Perhaps it had been lying underground for a hundred years or more. Now the woodchuck had given it to Alice.

Cousin Martha must have thought so, too, for when Alice offered it to her, she gave her a kind little look and took it. When Alice saw it again, it was set in a narrow silver rim and hung on a silver chain wrapped up in rose-colored cotton in a jeweler's box addressed to Alice. But that was nearly three weeks later. For the present, Alice walked up the hill happy enough to have found anything so beautiful and to have done her duty toward a guest whom she liked.

Cousin Martha had handed the little arrowhead to Raymond to look at and he held it in his brown hand gazing down at it intently.

"It was for birds," he said. His hand seemed to understand the arrow as though it had made it. Then he gave it back to Cousin Martha who wrapped it in a clean handkerchief and put it in her purse.

Somehow, Alice always remembered Raymond standing in the green lane with the white arrowhead in his hand. But there was to be another picture of him that was even clearer.

The stove at her home was kept in the summer kitchen and the great original fireplace was still used in the winter kitchen, with pewter above it on the mantel. On cool evenings, Olga would put in a billet or two of applewood to make the room cheerful.

One evening Alice's father went out to the sink to get a glass of water. When he came back to the library he had a mysterious look.

"Come," he said to Alice and her mother, "and don't say anything."

Both on tiptoe they followed him across the hall and the wainscoted dining room and waited while he softly lifted the latch.

Olga had gone upstairs and the room was almost dark, but a few tongues of flame pulsed in the fireplace, and outlined a dark figure stretched in a blanket on the hearth. Alice could hear the soft rustle of the fire and Raymond's quiet, slow breathing. They stood gazing for a moment and then tiptoed away.

"Now," said her father, "you, too, have seen an Indian asleep by the kitchen fire, Alice. Remember it when you read about the old days. They're never quite dead. The same things happen over and over. And Raymond's blanket, too, is part of an old, old story—it's a treaty blanket, you know, and the government still gives them every year—so many blankets, so much flour and gunpowder, in return for an old peace. Do remember, Alice!"

"Of course I'll remember," said Alice a little indignantly.

Raymond, to her, was something wonderful, a sort of kind, matter-of-fact ghost who had stepped into their lives. He might disappear at any moment.

And, in fact, that is exactly what Raymond did do. After a few weeks, when he had finished all the small things that were to be done about the place, he seemed to grow restless.

"I'd better be going along, now," he said one day to Alice's father. "Sometime I'll come back. You're good people here."

And sure enough, Raymond came back every year and spent a few days with Alice's family, in the kitchen ell that had known his ancestors, too, like some migrating bird which knows that in a certain spot it will meet with a welcome and a safe place in which to rest from the storm.

If you could see, if you could see,
If you could see the white canoes
Pulled up the beach, where oysters lay
Gathered in heaps for all to choose—

If round the tribal campfires you
Could hear the easy laughter ring,
While winter hunger was forgot
In the fat feasting of the spring—

If you could see, if you could hear,
You, too, might feel a fierce joy burn
At seeing grass turn green again
And watching the first birds return.

II

BROWNIE OF THE CIRCUS

ONCE a summer the circus came to Damariscotta and pitched its tent in Long's field above the river. It was a small circus, "like a big family," the circus people always said, but there were two elephants, and trained ponies, acrobats, and a little Wild West show, with a young man in a big hat who could lasso a running horse, or shoot cards out of his wife's hand.

This year there was an Indian family, too. Alice had seen their pictures, all in buckskin and feathers, and a little boy and girl who did Indian dances, though they looked younger than she was.

Alice and Marcia, her best friend, talked for a week about the Indian children. Marcia was sure that they could speak English like anyone else, but Alice said that until she heard them for herself she would believe that they spoke in the Indian language and made mysterious signs.

It was just the time for blueberries, which next to wild-strawberry time, is almost the nicest of the summer. Marcia and Alice could talk and talk as they gathered blueberries on the hillsides overlooking the town. They both hated gathering peas or beans, but there was something lovely and wild about blueberries. You could eat as many as you liked, for one thing; and then there were the smells of sweet fern and sunny dry earth, and the wind, and the town lying in a hollow below you, with the great river flowing through it, and best of all there was excitement. You knew where peas or beans were going to be, but no one had planted blueberries. They grew here, they grew there; sometimes a bush would have scarcely a berry on it, then another would be so full of them that the children had only to run their hands down the twigs to fill them with dark-blue fruit.

Nothing seemed quite real from the sunny hillslopes. Sometimes the air moved up and down in the heat; sometimes Alice would think so hard about things that they would seem to come real and an acrobat all in white tights and spangles would seem standing on one foot on the steeple of the Congregational church; or two elephants, with the second holding the other one's tail with his trunk, would march down the main street far below them.

Once the elephants seemed so real that Alice pointed them out to Marcia. But Marcia, of course, didn't see them and only thought that Alice was fooling. And Alice was, in a way; but in another way she wasn't.

The day of the circus was as warm and bright as all the other days had been. The first show didn't begin until three o'clock, but Alice and Marcia couldn't wait that long. They went over to Long's meadow the moment they had finished their lunches. They wore their best ginghams and their hats. Their hair was freshly brushed, and yellow braids and brown braids shone in the sunlight. But the really important thing was that each had a new crinkly dollar bill in her pocketbook.

There were not many people near the tent so early in the afternoon, but the ponies were there with their master, four of them, tied to the fence, waiting for someone to ride them. Alice immediately liked the pony at the end of the line best. He was small, with pretty legs and hoofs and a white star on his forehead, but he drew back his ears along his neck and rolled his eyes at the children as they came near.

"Brownie is a little cranky today," the owner of the ponies said. "You little girls had better try Nip and Tuck. They're always gentle and willing."

But as Alice rode Nip down the paddock and back again, she was still thinking of Brownie and his pretty, unhappy look.

"I *know* I could make friends with him," she said, as she and Marcia rode knee to knee on their second ride.

"With whom?" said Marcia.

"Brownie," said Alice. "I love him."

14

"Well, I love Tuck, don't I, Tuck?" said Marcia, leaning forward to pat her pony's sturdy neck. Marcia was a wise little girl and always liked what she already had, but Alice's likings were like birds that settled down on any bough that pleased them. She patted Nip, too, but absent-mindedly, for she was imagining herself on Brownie, galloping very fast before a prairie fire, perhaps carrying a warning to people, too, that some enemy was planning to surprise them.

When Nip ambled to a halt at the rail, she looked up surprised.

"Let's get an ice-cream cone now," said Marcia.

"You get two and I'll stay here until you come back." Alice was standing near Brownie, but not looking at him.

"You look out, miss, that pony don't give you a nip," warned the man.

"Oh, he won't," answered Alice with assurance.

"Well, don't come hollering to me if he does," said the man rather disagreeably.

While Marcia was gone, Alice moved a little nearer Brownie and began saying quietly, "Good Brownie, there's a good horse. Good Brownie." She took care to make no sudden moves and she talked in a low, singsong voice. No one had ever told her to do these things, but she felt inside her that a horse would like to be treated that way. Out of the corner of her eye she could see that Brownie's ears were prick-

15

ing toward her, as though he were interested, but just then a big boy came, chose Brownie, and rode off. Alice watched. The pony was all right until the boy kicked him in the ribs, then he laid back his ears and bucked. The boy stuck on and kicked him harder. Brownie turned around and tried to bite his rider's leg, but by then the man in charge had run up, and hit his muzzle with a stick.

"Oh, poor Brownie!" said Marcia, suddenly appearing out of nowhere with an ice-cream cone in each hand.

Alice said nothing, though she opened her mouth to speak and then shut it. She watched with angry eyes while the boy finished his ride, kicking triumphantly. Brownie's ears were back, his eyes were rolled till they showed their whites, but he trotted sulkily about the usual course, and then came to a sudden halt at the hitching post.

When the boy had gone away, Alice took the cone which Marcia was still holding for her, and began to eat it. It was melting, so she ate fast, but absent-mindedly, her eyes still on Brownie.

By this time music had begun in the tent, and people were going in. The show would soon begin: no one was stopping to look at ponies when there were elephants somewhere, and trained monkeys, clowns, and acrobats in tights. The ringmaster came to the entrance and began calling,

"Come in, ladies and gentlemen, the show will begin in

"I am going to stay out here with Brownie"

five minutes. Come in, and get the best seats; the show will begin in a few minutes."

Marcia tugged at Alice's arm. "Come on, Alice, the show is going to begin!"

And the drums tugged, too, in their way saying, "Hurry up, hurry up, hurry up, Alice."

But Alice shook her head, a little impatiently. "You go in, Marcia," she said. "I'm going to stay out here with Brownie."

"But it won't be any fun all alone," said Marcia, looking very disappointed.

"I'm sorry, Marcia, but I just can't."

Marcia and Alice had been best friends for a long time. So Marcia knew from Alice's voice that she would never change her mind. Alice was that way; usually she did whatever other people wanted, but once in a while she didn't. And this was one of those times.

Just then some of the other children in their class at school came by and Marcia asked if she might go along with them. Then Alice was left alone to finish her ice-cream cone and talk to Brownie.

She had a lovely hour. It was a real adventure. The sun was very bright, and the river seemed bluer than she had ever seen it. A little breeze moved among the trees and kept the balloons swaying above the balloon stand. From the big tent

19

near by came music and applause. The man in charge of the ponies sometimes told her what was happening: "That's the elephants" or perhaps, "Guess Bill's been doing that new stunt on the trapeze." She had seen the circus several times and could guess what was happening inside. And it made her feel almost like being one of the circus people herself to be sitting here on the fence, with the sun warm across her shoulders, talking to the pony man. Once the woman who sold hot dogs, pop, and ice cream came and talked for a few minutes; and once the two little Indian children in buckskin and beadwork came and stared at her from friendly black eyes, after they had finished their dance.

But though Alice was pleasantly aware of all these things, yes, and of the smells of peanuts and wild animals and hot dust, it was Brownie that she was busy with all the time; it was Brownie to whom she sat nearer and nearer, and for whom she bought apples, and to whom she talked mostly; and when after nearly twenty minutes she began to pet him quietly, he did not lay back his ears, nor show his teeth.

"May I ride him?" Alice asked a little later.

The man pushed back his cap and looked at her. "I see you understand horses," he said. "You try, and I'll keep an eye on you in case there's any trouble."

Alice hadn't had much experience with horses, so she felt very proud, but she had a feeling of what it must be like to be an animal. She got into the saddle slowly. She didn't pull on the bit: Brownie had been jerked at by so many inexperienced hands. She didn't kick him in the ribs either: so many hard little heels had thumped against his sides. Alice could feel down to her bones just how sick of it all he was.

So she let him take his own time going from the bar, and she tried to fit her body into his, and for the first time around the course she let him walk. But the second time around she gave a little chirrup to him, and to her delight he broke into a trot of his own accord; and later on when she chirruped again he went very fast, and then Alice found that riding was easy.

She leaned forward and patted Brownie's neck; she called him a beauty. She held the reins just tight enough to feel his mouth in case he stumbled. But Brownie didn't stumble. He galloped. Alice's braids flew out, her hat fell off, her cheeks turned red as roses, her eyes shone with excitement. This was easiest of all. This was like flying. It seemed to her that the sound of Brownie's hoofs was part of the beating of her own heart.

But Alice had only a dollar altogether. She kept count of the number of times she went around the course, and when she had used up the amount she drew in sadly enough beside Nip and Tuck and their owner.

"Well," he said, "you're the first person besides my son

21

Tim I ever saw to get on with Brownie. He's too nervous for this work. It keeps me busy seeing no one gets hurt, and Tim's everlastingly after me to let him have Brownie for his own. But he'd be a dandy pony if I can break him to this work, and I never yet failed to break a pony."

"How long have you been trying?" asked Alice, feeling sadder. "And is he better?"

"Two years, and he's worse. But I mean to keep at it," said the man with a scowl, holding Brownie's bit as Alice dismounted. He took her money and dropped it into his pocket. Then he lighted a cigarette. The band was still playing from the tent, but the shadows were lengthening across the fields and the gulls were drifting up river with the tide.

Alice was pulling long grass for Brownie. The man watched her for a minute, and a pleasant grin came over his face.

"Look here," he said, "I'm just going to use Nip and Tuck after the people start coming out. There won't be many wanting to ride, anyhow. Why don't you take Brownie down to the end of the field and back, if you'd like to?"

"I haven't any money," said Alice.

"I know that," said the man. "That's all right."

Alice would never forget her feelings as the man swung open the gate of the inclosure and she passed through on Brownie's back. There was a farm lane along the edge of the

22

field above the river, which they reached after skirting the tent pins and motor vans of the circus. A goat baaed at her, and a woman waved, who was sitting in the sun with a dressed-up monkey on her knees. Then Alice passed away from even the circus. In all the world there were only Brownie and Alice, moving along the empty lane. She chirruped, and Brownie broke into a trot and at last into a run. Alice thought Joan of Arc might have felt like that, charging.

The lane must have been nearly a third of a mile long. When they turned back, the village and even the circus seemed far away, but Alice pulled Brownie to a walk so that she might taste her pleasure for as long as possible. She was still in the saddle when the people began coming out of the tent's entrance, and she found Marcia looking for her.

"It was wonderful!" said Marcia. "Oh, Alice, you missed everything!"

Alice leaned down smiling and patted Brownie's neck. "Do you see that hedge?" she asked. "We galloped all the way. And Brownie understands every word I say to him, don't you, Brownie?"

Brownie may not have understood, but he nickered after Alice, as she tore herself away, and then laid back his ears as someone else came too near his head. One of his hind hoofs was resting lightly, ready for a kick, and there was a wicked look in his eye.

23

"Don't seem like the same pony," thought his master, without his usual annoyance.

He looked meditatively down the empty lane and saw a vision of brown braids flying above a little galloping horse.

And as he unhitched Nip for the next rider, he made up his mind at last. "Tim shall have the obstinate little beast," he thought. "It's a real pity to see him spoiled at work he was never meant for."

What is once loved
You will find
Is always yours
From that day.

Take it home
In your mind
And nothing ever
Can **steal it away.**

III

A PICNIC AT THE MANSION

EVERY fine Saturday morning Olga put up a picnic lunch for three, neatly packed away in the old covered basket that Alice's grandmother had bought from the Indians who in those days sold their work from door to door. Alice loved to watch the bright-blue beetleware cups and plates, the curious knubby parcels done up in wax paper, and the salad bowl with the nasturtiums on it tucked each into its place by Olga's quick fingers. Olga never forgot anything, not even salt, nor the fresh-picked sprigs of marjoram for the top of the salad.

26

She kept her mind on what she was doing, not like Alice whose mind half the time seemed to be on something else.

When the picnic basket was all packed, Olga went out and rang the ship's bell that hung near the kitchen door, and then Alice's father got up from his knees beside the herb garden where he had been doing some late weeding, and Alice's mother at her desk hastily finished a letter and addressed its envelope, and Alice very carefully carried the big basket and then the thermos bottles out to the car, and they were off for another day of exploration.

They usually all sat on the front seat together because it was so much cozier that way, and they explored forgotten roads. They chose roads with scarcely any wheel marks on them, where the trees nearly met overhead, and on these roads they made many discoveries. They found streams nearly choked with the brilliance of cardinal flowers, and old mills with their roofs falling in and their walls half rotted away and their great stones thrown down which had once ground so much corn into meal and so much wheat into flour for the earlier settlers. They found the cellar holes of old houses on little coves of the salt rivers with the water sparkling beyond them and the lilacs clustered by the burnt chimneys and the pink Bouncing Bet growing wild among the grasses like friends who had never forgotten the hands that first planted them so long ago.

Once they came on a little old house in the deep woods where ancient apple trees grew high among the pines and the tumbled stone walls circled nothing but woodlands where someone had once had rye fields and pasture land. But the little house was freshly painted and there were bright petunias growing in green tubs on either side of the door. There was a little lawn tucked up close to its green door and the windows were shining. But there was no one there at all, and Alice named it the House of the Three Bears.

Their favorite road was a ridge road over the river with old pine trees growing above the walls like rows of giants, and occasional farms still occupied. They did old-fashioned things on these farms: planted little strips of garden by the side of the road for the passers-by to enjoy; used oxen for plowing and drawing the blue hay carts; and dried hand-dipped candles from the beams of their sheds where the yellow seed corn hung. Not, of course, that every farm did all these things, but each farm did one or another of them. You might even see a hen with her chicks about her, which is a very rare sight in the country in these days of incubators.

On this August Saturday the men were out cutting the hay on the sloping fields that stretched down to the river, and Alice and her father and mother waved to them all and everyone waved back good-naturedly to them. But there was an air of hurry in the fields, for the day which had begun so

28

sunnily was growing overcast, and the big white clouds had somehow turned black and stood up like a dark wall in the northwest, against which the woods and fields shone bright emerald. A little thunder began like the rattle and rumble of a hay wagon over a bridge.

Alice's mother, who never cared for storms, suggested that perhaps they had better be going home, but her father shook his head.

"We shan't be able to make it," he said, "it's coming fast. Hear the leaves rustle already. Perhaps we'd better try to go on to the Mansion."

"It may go round," said Alice's mother hopefully.

But the storm had no intention of going around. Fast as they drove, they had just reached the big square empty house with its sagging verandahs when the leaves began to rustle and whisper, "Rain, rain, rain," and then the sun suddenly disappeared and the first slow drops began to fall, and then there came a flash of lightning and a clap of near-by thunder and the rain began to fall faster and faster.

It certainly seemed a very bad day for a picnic.

"Perhaps we'd better eat our lunch on the verandah," Alice's father suggested. "There's going to be a regular downpour, I'm afraid." So while there was still time they each seized something and ran toward the house.

But the rain fell more and more heavily and splashed into

29

the open verandah, and the thunder and lightning crashed and flared above them, and Alice and her father and mother looked as dismal as three cats on a doorstep in a shower. Her father had begun poking and prying at the windows of the old house and all of a sudden he shouted:

"Hurrah! Here's an open one!" and held it up while Alice and her mother and the picnic basket and the thermos bottles were all lifted in, and then he came in, too.

They had climbed into the kitchen: the stove was there, and broken dishes on the sink, and an old calendar of many years ago hung on the wall. The house smelled unused. They tiptoed into the next room. There was no furniture in it, except a clock that had lost its pendulum. But the parlor still had its rose-flowered carpet tacked on the floor, and there were still steel engravings of a congress of American authors, and of St. Cecilia and a Landseer stag. Someone had tumbled most of the books out of the shelves on one side of the fireplace, but there was a haircloth sofa and chairs with grape ornaments, and in the corner between the windows stood a little flat-topped organ, with old music still on its rack.

The rest of the house was almost empty except for big beds too heavy to carry away and pictures that nobody wanted, but it had an air of dignity and its old wallpapers had been there since before the Civil War, Alice's father said.

Outside, the lightning and thunder had increased and the

rain turned the windowpanes gray with the streams of water running down the glass. Alice went into the kitchen and came back with some old wooden boxes she had found.

"Let's make a fire, Father," she said.

"Would it be right?" asked her mother, looking very cold in her damp summer dress.

Alice's father made up his mind quickly. "I can't see that it would do any harm," he said. "The chimneys seem sound."

In five minutes the parlor of the Mansion had become a real refuge against the storm. A small fire crackled and spat out sparks from the old fireplace (Alice put them out when they fell on the carpet) and the books were put back onto the shelves, and while her mother laid the marble-topped table with the checked red and white table cloth from the picnic basket, her father played Scotch songs on the little sweet-voiced organ, which Alice liked better than any piano she had ever seen or heard, even though it was somewhat out of tune.

"Luncheon is served," said her mother, and they all pulled up chairs and began eating hungrily.

"It's like being someone else," remarked Alice dreamily. "It's all so *secret*, like an enchanted house. I wonder who lived here?"

But they never knew.

After lunch they explored the sheds that opened out from

31

the kitchen and found a broom made from a single piece of birch, with its end sliced into hundreds of splinters and tied together, so that broom and handle were all one.

"An Indian broom," Alice's father said. "I've heard that the squaws used to sell one for nine-pence, though they took a long time to make."

There were cheese-making things, too, and a spinning wheel and loom, and a cobbler's bench with wooden feet hanging on the wall near by so that the traveling shoemaker could use them for fitting shoes for the whole family during the days he lived at the house, once or twice a year. One of the pairs of feet was just the size of Alice's, but whether they had been a little boy's or a little girl's was another of the things she never knew.

By this time the storm had lifted and there was a rainbow over the pines and the leaves were dripping with drops that caught in the new sunlight.

Alice's father carefully put out the fire and then took the paper bag that had had three peaches in it and wrote a note on it to whomever the house belonged to, explaining who they were and how they had happened to break in where only spiders were at home. But what else he wrote in the note Alice never knew until Christmas morning when she woke up to hear "O Little Town of Bethlehem" being played very sweetly and softly in her own playroom, and so went flying out of bed without her slippers or wrapper, with her brown hair unbraided and her eyes half blind with sleep to throw her arms about her father and welcome the little organ from the Mansion which had come to be her very own, all in tune now, with her name on an ivory heart set into the wood just above the old keys.

In fury and terror
The tempest broke;
It tore up the pine
And shattered the oak,

Yet the hummingbird hovered
Within the hour,
Sipping clear rain
From a trumpet flower.

IV

CALYPSO

ALTHOUGH Alice was very fond of animals, she had none of her own. Her father thought that dogs barked a good deal and kept things in an uproar. Her mother didn't want a cat to catch the birds and scare away the chipmunks, so Alice, as I said, had no animals of her own.

Alice was a quiet child with a bang of dark hair and two small braids tied with red ribbon, who went about with her thoughts often in a dream; and often her dreams were of the sea, for twice every day the great salt tides of the ocean poured up the river on which the town where she lived was built and spread inland like a flood of green glass, and twice every day the tides raced down the river to the sea once more. Alice was accustomed to the smell of salt water mixed with the scent of her mother's garden, and nearly every day of her life she saw sea gulls perched on the roofs of the brick stores that lined the main street of the town.

The house, too, reminded her of the sea, for there were

two shells at the door with pink mouths and the wallpaper in the dining room had been captured from an English vessel sailing to the West Indies during the War of 1812.

Beyond the old orchard was a little cove, which was almost dry at low tide, and the water coming in over the sunwarmed mud flats was good for swimming. Alice had absent-mindedly learned to swim very well, and she could row a small dory and scarcely know she was doing it. She had noticed which way the wind was blowing and how the tides were running before she could read the alphabet. Everyone she knew looked at the weathervane before he looked at the morning paper. They were part of life, like the sun and rain. Where Alice lived the land and sea were neighbors.

One summer evening Alice's father and mother were away. She had her supper early, a chop and string beans, milk and brownbread and jam from the wild strawberries she herself had picked in the hayfields. The dishes she used had come from England and were part of Great-grandmother Prescott's dowry; the silver spoon with the dent in it had been buried long before under a log-house doorstep when the Indians were about to attack the settlement.

After supper Alice wandered into the garden. The setting sun shone across the flowers full into the face of a moon rising very round and large over the pines of Tuesday Point. The sun and moon seemed staring quietly at each other across

Alice was dreaming as she rowed out and caught the current

Alice. She felt rather lonely with her family away and wandered down to the cove without thinking about it. She saw that the tide was still running toward the sea, but would soon be turning again.

Alice was an obedient child, but she was absent-minded. As she got into the dory and rattled the oars into the oarlocks she was thinking about a poem.

> "*The moon on one hand*
> *And the sun on the other,*
> *The moon is my sister,*
> *The sun is my brother,*"

was the way she remembered it. She was not thinking about rowing at all, nor about her father's rule that she must never go out on the river alone, and must be home before dark. Alice was dreaming as she rowed out and caught the current; it needed only a little steering on her part to be carried along swiftly, by the shore edged with a white rim of boulders, with pines sometimes overhanging the water and sometimes fields of stubble.

Alice faced the town and the setting sun. As she half drifted and half rowed, the buildings grew smaller and the sun sank from sight among a great swirl of clouds like wings, very rosy. But for all their rosiness Alice felt over her shoulder the white light of the moon streaming past her, and gradually the cloud wings turned ashy and stars appeared between the feathers; but the cool white light of the moon grew brighter and brighter and danced on the water and lighted the leaves to a dull soft green and shone dim red on Alice's dress.

A bend in the river hid the town; far off she could see the wink of automobile lights like glaring beads strung along a road no wider than a thread. The lisp of the water against the sides of her boat, the kind, quiet help of the tide that seemed to have set its shoulder to the dory stern and be pushing it along, kept Alice in her daydream.

A great heron rose from a boulder and flew almost overhead, its wings flapping very slowly, its legs trailing gracefully behind it. Alice was used to herons, but its rising up so near her brought her back to herself.

"I've gone far enough," she thought hastily. "I'd better get back before Olga misses me. Father wouldn't like this a bit," and she tried to turn the dory into the oncoming tide.

But though a man might have succeeded, making use of the slow currents by the shore, Alice didn't have the strength. The water kept its great shoulder to the dory like a genie which had been released from his bottle and knew that no one remembered the spell to make him go back.

"It will turn soon," thought Alice, giving up the struggle. "Mercy! I'm almost at Seal Rocks."

But now Alice no longer moved in a dream of moonlight. She kept thinking how upset her father and mother would be if they came home before she did. In her anxious state she noticed everything; the little cool breeze that had sprung up; the chirping of the crickets from the stubble; the leaping of the fish in their widening silver circles. A round velvet head appeared and dark eyes looked at her; then another. She was abreast Seal Rocks, and the seals, too, were awake. She could see them crawling clumsily along the beach or playing in the moonlit water; they seemed to take her boat for a large seal and sported about it, swimming close without any fear.

Alice knew that the fishermen sometimes fed the seals and that some of them were very tame. She could find only a little bait in a pail, but she threw that to them and they ate it greedily.

At last the tide turned, and Alice, too, turned the dory and started home. Now she faced into the moon which was much higher in the sky than it had been when she started, and smaller and brighter. It was not so magical; it was more like a bright lamp held in unseen hands. Anyway, it was lighting home a disobedient little girl and Alice was grateful to it.

Up the river went the tide from the great plains of the sea, carrying with it Alice and the dory. And behind the

dory came the seals, at first all of them, and finally only two
or three. Alice sang to them:

> "*Row, row, row your boat*
> *Gently down the stream,*
> *Merrily, merrily, merrily, merrily,*
> *Life is but a dream,*"

and "Jolly boating weather," keeping time with her oars.

At last, over her shoulder, she could see the lights of the
town and the little bristling lights of the cars, and then she
heard the bell of the red church booming, ding dong, ding
dong, very, very slowly—seven o'clock, eight o'clock, nine
o'clock, surely it would stop now, but no, ten o'clock. Her
mother and father would be wild.

She rowed hard now, adding her strength to the strength
of the sea. When she thought about the seals again, they were
all gone but one. It was cold, and a mist was beginning to
rise. Alice was wide awake. When she reached the cove, she
saw that the house was full of lights—her family were home
and looking for her. Across the still air she heard a telephone
bell jangle and then the door opened on a flood of light and
a figure hurried out toward the car.

"Father!" she called. "Father! I'm down here tying up
the boat!"

Her father turned and ran toward her through the apple
trees.

42

He was shaking her by the shoulders. "Alice! Alice! What do you mean? On the river at this time of night all by yourself?"

"But I wasn't all by myself," said Alice, saying anything that came into her head. "There was the seal."

Her father's eye followed Alice's small pointing finger. Sure enough, there was a round velvet head and two eyes shining in the moonlight. The seal opened its mouth and barked throatily, rolled slowly out of sight, stuck up his head in a new place, and barked again.

"Quick, run up and see if Olga hasn't some fish in the ice box," said Alice's father, forgetting to scold just then.

And that is how Calypso happened to come to the cove and stay there and move flip flop up through the orchard to the kitchen door when she was hungry, and swim all about Alice when she swam on warm days.

And though, of course, her father and mother spoke seriously to Alice about forgetting what people told her not to do, they were so charmed with Calypso and her friendly coaxing ways that they couldn't scold very much.

And, really, Alice was much better after that night and the coming of a gift from the sea and the moon. She was so busy playing with Calypso and with all the children who came to see Calypso that she forgot some of her old day-dreaming ways; her smooth dark head with its brown bangs

43

and small red-ribboned braids moved about as busily as anyone's, and she remembered what people told her to do and
not to do.

As for Calypso, she grew fatter and fatter, for she had only
to bark and someone was sure to throw her a mackerel or a
slice of fish. It was hard to believe that one young seal could
ever eat all that Calypso managed to eat.

But everyone was well pleased: Alice and her father and
mother, who had a playmate from the sea; Calypso, who was
fat and merry with so much food; and the man with the
fishcart who stopped morning and afternoon at the kitchen
door and smiled with satisfaction as he made out his bill at the
end of the month.

Mighty are the rivers
Flowing to the sea,
With the. islands in their channels
And the ocean at their doors.
The thrushes and the bobolinks
And sea gulls all agree
As neighbors of the rivers
Meeting along their shores.

Mighty are the rivers
And wide and dark they flow,
Down from the fields and forests,
Down to meet the tide.
Only the old remember,
Only the old men know
How once the sailing vessels
Sailed down them in their pride!

V

FAIR DAY

IT WAS when the year was at its best, when the summer people were gone, and the ladders leaned against the apple trees, and the bluebirds were calling their lovely autumn call, and all the woods looked golden and bronze as though they had grown in the valleys of the sun—it was then when the world was at its nicest that every year the county fair was held. Alice had heard about the fair all her life,

46

but she had never been taken to it for her mother thought she was too young to be in such a crowd. But at last came the year when she was old enough to go.

For days beforehand Alice watched the weather, begrudging the beautiful days for fear they were storing up rain, afraid when it rained that a long autumn storm had begun which might last for days. Everyone else was watching the weather in just the same way, in town and on all the farms. The fair was the great occasion of the year when people saw their friends who lived in remote places and whom, perhaps, they never saw at other times.

The day before the fair opened was misty and wet. Everyone kept an anxious eye on the weathervanes and hoped the wind would swing landward in an orderly clockwise fashion. Alice wore her rubbers and red raincoat to school; she felt very gloomy. At supper time it was still raining, a rain that was half fog, like wet cotton wool. Alice's father still hoped the wind might shift, but the floors were cold, and between the windows and the street lights there was a continual curtain of almost soundless rainfall.

That evening Alice's father lighted a fire of old apple logs in the fireplace and Alice brought her book near it to read. Her mother was embroidering.

"I saw some of the fair trucks go through today," she said.

Alice looked up, brightening a little.

"One was the merry-go-round, I'm sure," her mother went on, "and there were several of the caravan automobiles with curtains at the windows. And do you know, one had a canary cage hanging between the curtains. It must seem strange to have your house always on wheels, never in one place for more than two or three nights."

Alice thought of the caravan houses camped now only a few miles away, but she could feel the cold rain dripping, dripping from their roofs. And inside them there were cross and discouraged people. It was going to rain forever and her first fair day would be spoiled. She felt sorry for everyone, but oh, sorriest of all for Alice who had been looking forward so long to the fair!

Just then there was a knock at the door and her father went to answer it. Alice could hear a stranger's voice, deep and drawling, and her father's voice answering, very friendly and interested. They talked for some little while and Alice could not help wondering who had come. Then her father called over his shoulder.

"Do come here, both of you, and meet Mr. Dunbar, and see what he has with him."

Alice and her mother both went, and there at the door stood an elderly man with clear blue eyes in a thin wrinkled face. He shook hands with them. His hand was cold and wet with rain. Behind him in the light of the street lamp stood two yoke of oxen, their heads patiently lowered, their slow breath making a thicker fog in the quiet rain. One pair were very large brown and white animals with a yoke painted carriage blue, and brass balls at the ends of their horns. The others were smaller and the color of oak leaves or kelp.

"Mr. Dunbar stopped to ask the way to the fair grounds," explained Alice's father. "I told him it was still some distance and we had room in the barn for his oxen and—" his eye caught the eye of Alice's mother.

"And Mr. Dunbar will stay with us," she said warmly. "Have you had your dinner yet, Mr. Dunbar? Olga will have something hot ready for you in two minutes."

Mr. Dunbar hesitated, but Alice's family was so insistent, and surely a warm bed seemed better than sleeping in the straw of the cattle shed on such a night. Alice, greatly excited, went out to the barn with him and her father, while he bedded the big oxen in the old unused stalls that stretched beyond the one where Bessie, the Jersey cow, stood. It seemed beautiful to see so many large calm creatures together, and to be allowed to pet the matted curls between their horns, and let them lick salt from the palm of her hand, while their shadows moved among the disused cobwebs.

When Mr. Dunbar had eaten his supper he, too, came in to sit by the fire. He had changed his clothes and wore newly blackened shoes. He didn't seem tired, although he

49

and the oxen had walked for two days now, slowly, slowly along the sides of the roads while the cars went by.

"When you have a pretty good yoke," he explained, "you like to see how they measure up with the others. Oxen aren't as common as they used to be. I can remember when it wasn't unusual to see six yoke hauling a mast, and my grandfather used to say that when *he* was a boy you'd see fifty yoke; yes, a hundred oxen, hauling one big piece of timber out of the woods—first-growth pine of course and sometimes five feet across at the butt. It must have been a very fine sight."

Alice's father asked him many questions. Mr. Dunbar liked to talk about oxen.

"I've never been much of a horse man," he said. "I guess I'm a little scared of horses."

He told them how an ox can go through deep snow much better than a horse, and how you can tell he is tired when he lolls out his tongue; he told them about training the calves and of the various methods different men used with their creatures.

After a little talk he said shyly to Alice's mother, "Would you mind if I whittle a little? Now my daughter is married I live by myself and sometimes evenings I make things for the grandchildren. I have something with me that's almost finished which I'd like to leave for the little girl here, but it needs another hour's work."

Mr. Dunbar went out to his wagon and brought back a rather damp shoe box. Alice waited to see what was in it, trying to be polite and not too eager. Then in the firelight Mr. Dunbar brought out a perfect little hay wagon with spoked wheels, and set it on the hearth. Next came a pair of little oxen about five inches long made of whittled and smoothed pine, with coarse string tails frayed out at the end. The little oxen stood patiently just as the real oxen had stood among the wet leaves by the side of the road, and their horns went up in the same curve from their broad smooth pine foreheads.

Alice's mother clapped her hands.

"What a beautiful thing it is, Mr. Dunbar! It's more than a toy, it's a real piece of art like a painting."

A very pleased look came into Mr. Dunbar's eyes. "I got the idea from something I found in the attic chamber which must have been there from before my grandfather's time," he said.

Alice didn't go to bed until the small dark yoke had been whittled and sand-papered and fitted to the oxen and the cart thill. As she watched Mr. Dunbar's quiet clever hands she made up her mind that she would learn to do something, embroider like her mother or paint—anyway, something to make her hands look alive like Mr. Dunbar's. When the little hay wagon and oxen stood all finished on the mantel,

Alice gave him a kiss. She would never see fog and rain again without thinking of oxen: great oxen gently breathing in the night rain; little oxen standing in the firelight.

When she woke up next morning Mr. Dunbar was already gone. Only the toy oxen on the mantel showed that last night had not all been a dream. The wind had shifted and the clouds moved in cheerful flocks on the horizon, leaving the sun to shine and dazzle the wet polished leaves of the trees and the wet bending blades of grass.

By ten o'clock Alice and her father and mother were leaving their car in a field and joining all the other people crowding toward the fair grounds. Once through the gate, amid all the hullabaloo of calliopes and barkers, they passed down a double row of booths and sideshows behind which Alice could catch glimpses of the caravans. Beyond the circus flags flapped rather worn underclothing on lines.

Alice saw everything in rather exciting snatches. She was too old to be carried on her father's shoulders and too small to see very well unless she got to the edge of the crowd. But the crowd was part of the excitement: coats and skirts, bright and dull, all shifting around her, and the ground covered with shoes of every size and pattern, all moving, and overhead a network of voices that never stopped. And over that, again, the shrill music and the tired insistent voices calling, "Come in, folks! see all the strange people: the freaks and the curiosities"—"This way, folks! a real live gorilla out of the jungles"—"Three balls for a dime! Three balls for a dime!"—"The hand is quicker than the eye." . . .

Alice threw some wooden rings until one went over a handle ("Ten cents! Play until you win!") and she won a ring that looked like silver set with a sapphire. She went on the merry-go-round, choosing a very wild-looking mustang to ride, but before she had been around twice she felt rather sick at her stomach, and shut her eyes except when she opened them to smile at her father and mother who were standing near the booth waiting for her. She was very glad when at last the music stopped grinding and she could get off. There were some very big, rather soiled posters of a boa constrictor strangling an ox on the pampas and of a baboon in a jungle tree, but when they went into the tent they found two small monkeys in a cage and a few snakes no bigger than walking sticks. But the monkeys were very friendly. Alice liked their little sad eyes so close together that they made her think of a cocoanut; and there was an exhibit of white mice, too, with a tent of their own and little houses and trucks in which they climbed in and out. It made Alice wonder what a world of white mice would really be like if they behaved like people.

Alice's father won a fuzzy toy cat by hitting two wooden men off a shelf with his first two balls, and they all ate spun-sugar candy that was brittle and sweet and unsatisfying. The

53

midway was really very small. They soon were looking at White Laced Wyandotte hens and at pumpkins; then they drifted down to the race track. Beautiful horses were trotting around it; they were a little like waves and a little like engines. The elderly drivers wore faded silk jackets and yellow glasses, and called out to each other as they fought for the inside of the track. When a horse won, there was cheering from the grandstand. Alice's father took them back of the track to the little lean-tos where the horses and the stablemen slept; and Alice watched the harnessing. The horses were nervous and irritable, and pawed and laid back their ears while the buckles were being fastened and the straps carefully adjusted, but once their drivers were in their seats, they went off for the next race shining and eager.

But the thing they all wanted to see was the oxen in the middle of the racing ring, standing in pairs in their big open shed with their yokes (blue like Mr. Dunbar's or Indian red, or unpainted but time-polished) lying in the aisle in front of them. In the field men and boys stood by a fence watching the oxen in their pulling contests. They had great rocks piled up on a drag and the teams took turns hauling it through the rutted mud, their long backs rounding up under the strain, their heads low, and their shoulders taking the burden. Beyond the slow-moving oxen Alice could see the trotting horses in the ring flash by with wide nostrils. It was as though the farmers and the oxen were the center of a clock, solid and sure, and the horses and the motors beyond were the hands, moving quickly.

They waited until they saw Mr. Dunbar's yoke of brown and white oxen win the pulling contest. He was very un-hurried with them, and as calm as though he were all alone in one of his own fields hauling stone for a new foundation. But when he knew they had won he looked pleased again as he had when Alice's mother praised his whittling. They all shook hands with him and Alice had brought more salt for the oxen.

"Next year you must come again and stay with us," they all said, and he promised he would.

Alice was getting tired, and the rest of the afternoon became more and more blurred. She ate hot-dogs and popcorn and more candy because it was fair day: she had her tintype taken (but she moved) and her fortune told by a real gypsy in a red skirt with fifty-cent pieces and quarters pierced and fastened to ribbons braided in her hair. Every now and then the gypsy stopped telling Alice's fortune to scold or slap one of the wild-looking little children who played in and out of her tent, but she told Alice a very fortunate fortune. Perhaps she didn't know that she gave Alice the wrong change.

Alice drank root beer. A man went by quarreling with his wife. When Alice stopped near the booths she could not

55

help seeing how worn and dirty the cloth was, though it looked so gay at a distance. And hardly any of the people in them had nice eyes.

Alice was glad when her first fair day was over. She felt very queer inside her with all the strange things she had eaten, and very bewildered with all the noises, and not at all interested in the fluffy cats and yellow-haired dolls and red canes piled in her arms. It was time to go home.

But that night as she lay quietly in bed, with the square of moonlight showing in her open window and the smell of salt water drifting to her from the river, she saw the fair again in her mind's eye. She was standing watching Mr. Dunbar and his big oxen and again the bright horses flashed by in the outer ring, and beyond them was the midway, foreign-feeling and mysterious in spite of its shabbiness. Where would they all be tomorrow? How did they live? She felt again her first excitement in the crowd; her sense of the known and the unknown all stirring together, of eyes that looked at her which had come from faraway places, of the music beating and beating, and the balloon which had floated up against the blue sky.

Fair day! And next year she would go again. But of course she couldn't expect the weather ever to be quite so warm and bright, or anything so beautiful as Mr. Dunbar's oxen standing in the darkness and rain. Your first fair day must be the loveliest of all, thought Alice, sleepily content.

I know this wind
Is blowing away
The fair that was here
Just yesterday:

Oxen with yokes,
And the merry-go-round,
Barkers, and papers
That littered the ground,

The blonde girl in tights
Whom they bucksaw in halves,
The trainers and trotters,
The cows with their calves,

The housewives' exhibits,
The pumpkins and corn,
The booths with their velvets
So dirtied and worn,

The great ferris wheel,
The lifter of loads,
All, all of them blowing
Away down the roads—

Country and city,
The rustic and urban,
The grower of apples,
The sage in his turban,

Are all of them blowing
Fast, fast, fast,
Into their futures
And into our past.

VI

IN SEARCH OF COSTMARY

ALICE's mother had been busy for days putting her garden away for the winter.

"I do want a few more herbs next year," she said at lunch one Saturday. "I think I'll put a clump of Costmary by the kitchen step. Alice, should you like to walk up to Miss Susy's with me after lunch and get some?"

Alice always liked going to Miss Susy's shop which had once been a chicken house, and now stood, very neat and pretty by the highway, with a garden about it. Miss Susy sold plants and flowers, spreads, aprons, jellies, cookies, bric-a-brac found in old attics, and even long-haired kittens which were usually to be found tumbling about underfoot, or trying to climb up the screens, staring out at the passers-by from round fluffy faces whose eyes were still an innocent milk blue.

Alice found the kittens and some sugar cookies with raisins in their centers, but her mother didn't find any Costmary.

"I've never had any of that," said Miss Susy. "But, oh yes, I know it very well. My grandmother had it, and always called it Sweet Mary. Do you know, Mrs. Riggs," she went on, turning to a woman who had come in with a just-finished hooked rug wrapped up in brown paper, "do you know any-one round here who might have Sweet Mary?"

"I don't know that I do," said Mrs. Riggs thoughtfully. "What about Mrs. Tibbetts out on the Christmas Cove road? Her garden is just like it was in her mother's time."

Alice and her mother drove out along the Christmas Cove road to the Tibbetts farm, which was not very easy to find. But they found it in time and a thin woman in steel-rimmed spectacles met them at the kitchen door.

"Sweet Mary?" she repeated. "Sweet Mary? I don't know

as I know what plant you mean. Maybe it's what we always used to call Sweet Tongue around here. Has it a long leaf with a good smell to it, and small button-shaped yellowy-green flowers? Of course I know it, then, but my old roots died out two winters ago after those March blizzards. But you won't have any trouble getting some, I'm sure."

"But can you tell me who might have it?" asked Alice's mother.

"You might try Sally Hinks—Mrs. Hiram Hinks," said Mrs. Tibbetts. "Yes, she'd be likely to have some. Her aunt used to be very fond of Sweet Tongue tea, I remember, when there was grippe around. You'll find their house," and then Mrs. Tibbetts gave many directions that Alice's mother repeated.

A light haze was coming over the sky, as so often happens down by the sea. There were many tamaracks in the lowlands that began to look, now, as though they were made of yellow spiderwebs, but pricklier. They passed a stream with five white ducks under a willow tree. Finally, after much doubling and turning down sandy roads, they came to a postbox marked "Hiram Hinks."

Mrs. Hinks was not at home, but her oldest daughter took Alice's mother and Alice out into the garden to see if they could find what they wanted.

"Do you see some, Alice?" her mother asked.

"I don't know what it looks like, Mother," said Alice who was watching some late bees rather stiffly visiting some cosmos.

"Well, I don't see any either. Do you know who else might have some?" her mother asked.

"I'll ask Grandfather," said the little girl, leading them back to the kitchen where her grandfather sat in a rocking chair near the stove.

"Grandpa," the child shouted, coming close to his ear, "this lady wants some Sweet Tongue. Do you know if Aunt Mary's got any?"

"Sweet Tongue?" said the old man turning bright blue eyes toward Alice's mother. "Is that what we used to call Bible Leaf when I was a young man?"

"I guess so," said Alice's mother, nodding her head several times.

"I suppose that wasn't its real name," went on the old man, stuffing his pipe. "Excuse me not getting up, but my rheumatism's bad. But people, when I was young, used to use those long sweet-smelling leaves to mark their places in the Bible. Might find one in our old Bible now; shouldn't wonder."

"But has your daughter any Bible Leaf, do you think?" shouted Alice's mother.

"Shouldn't wonder," said the old man, smiling and nod-

61

ding. "Myrna, you tell them how to get to your Aunt Mary's. It isn't more than a couple of miles."

Once more Alice and her mother climbed into their seats. Once more they followed the sea-coast roads, mostly through scrubby woods, but now and then they caught a glimpse of the sea.

"I feel as though you and I were detectives," said Alice's mother. "Every place we go they give it a different name, and send us on to follow the clue somewhere else. I don't think we ought to go back and admit ourselves beaten, do you, Alice?"

Alice was perfectly contented to wander around just seeing things. They had passed a house with fishing nets spread out on the grass to dry, and a field where a yoke of red oxen were busy at fall plowing. The earth, as it turned under the share, shone in the sun almost like dark waves. Alice was in no hurry to get home.

They had forgotten to ask Aunt Mary's last name, so this time they could not find the house by the postbox. It was Alice who remembered something about a martin house. Sure enough, there were four of them on very long poles, looking much newer and better-painted than the little house banked with straw to which they belonged.

Aunt Mary was a fat woman, and as cheerful as she was fat. She must have been fond of animals for Alice counted seven gray cats, and a hound tied beside an overturned barrel which served him for kennel. It was the same hound which had dug up Aunt Mary's garden so she scarcely had a root left.

"You never saw such a dog for digging," she said. "But look around, look around. If you find what you want, you're welcome to it before that dog digs it up. What was it you said? Bible Leaf? What does it look like?"

Alice's mother patiently described the plant once more, for the fifth time.

Aunt Mary's eye brightened. "Oh, *now* I know what you mean. *We* always call it Lavender. Where I used to work, the lady put the dried leaves in with her linen. I don't think I have any, but you might look."

If there had ever been any Lavender, the hound had long since dug it up. Aunt Mary suggested several people who might have it over Winslow Mills way, but now a chill and dusk were coming into the air, and even Alice's mother felt a little discouraged as they drove home.

"All I hoped for was a little Costmary," she said, "but now I feel as though I had lost Sweet Mary, Sweet Tongue, Bible Leaf, and Lavender, too."

And then she made up a verse as she drove along:

> *"I've never heard the sorrows sung*
> *Of ladies who have lost Sweet Tongue,*

63

I've never heard them tell the grief
Of gardens without Bible Leaf,

But gard-e-ners grow quite contrary,
Robbed of Costmary and Sweet Mary,

And become furious, I aver,
Without their usual Lavender."

"What does it look like?" asked Alice.

"My poor child, haven't you heard me describing it all afternoon from door to door?" cried Alice's mother in despair.

"I was thinking—" said Alice.

"But why do you want to know now?" asked her mother.

"I was just wondering—" said Alice meekly.

"Well, it's a big plant, often as high as your head, with sweet-smelling leaves shaped like tongues. And its flowers aren't much but buttons. People used to plant it for its fragrance and I thought it was nearly as common as mint, but I seem to be wrong."

It was almost dark when they reached home.

"Did you find your Costmary?" called out Alice's father cheerfully from the living room, as they came in.

"No, we didn't," said her mother. "They sent us round and round and round like people in a fairy tale, and everyone called it by a different name, but we never found it. I'm awfully disappointed, aren't you, Alice?"

64

But Alice wasn't there.

"She must have gone upstairs to take off her things," said her mother.

But when Alice came into the room again, she was still in her hat and coat and her eyes were full of mischief and her hands were behind her back.

"What will you give me for what I have in my hands, Mother?" she asked.

"A kiss," said her mother.

"Oh, that isn't enough for what *I* have," said Alice. "It ought to be a king's treasure or something like that, but a pair of skates might do. No, Mother, I'm just teasing. Here it is," and she held up her hands filled with green, sweet-smelling leaves.

"Alice! *Where* did you get it?" cried her mother, in a rather weak voice. "Where in the world? Did you know all the time?"

"Of course not, Mother," said Alice giggling. "You didn't describe it to *me* until on the way home. And then I began to wonder if it wasn't the stuff that grew back of the orchard where the old hen houses used to be. Marcia and I call it Sachet Plant. We like the smell."

Still it is wilderness, strung with roads and farmsteads
Like necklaces of wampum; lonely still
Comes the loon's call; the deer slip through the thicket,
And the fox raises wild cubs on the hill.

Still grow the Indian crops, the corn and pumpkin,
As when the squaws tilled them with clam-shell spades,
And still the Indian ghosts return with autumn
To smoke their pipes among the forest glades.

VII

RAINY-DAY ATTIC

ONE of the places Alice loved to go was to Simeon Hall's junk shop, which was in a small red-brick building a little back from the main street. Simeon Hall was an old man with a wooden leg. He liked working in his garden better than sitting in his shop, so often Alice and her best friend Marcia would find a small sign pinned to the door, "Out back in the garden, S. H." and then they could either go out back and help Mr. Hall weed his vegetables, or walk into the shop and look at what was there.

It was not the kind of shop to attract summer people unless they were very wise and unhurried, but it was a place where a housewife could buy a secondhand kitchen stove good for another twenty years of baking pies and roasting meat, or a farmer might find a secondhand harness for his plowhorse, hanging from the cobwebby rafters. There was nothing so dusty, so cracked, or so worn that it didn't have a story and when Simeon Hall was in his shop he would tell some of these stories to the little girls.

Because Alice and Marcia were best friends they did their hair alike, but Marcia's bang and braids were as light as Alice's were dark, and her eyes were as blue as two morning-glories. But to keep her from being a picture child, she had a large gay mouth and freckles across her nose. She was more independent than Alice, but often Alice did things that Marcia wouldn't even have thought of, because it never occurred to her that they were brave or unusual. Alice looked best in red, and Marcia in blue, so at last, since they wished to be dressed like twins, their mothers bought them plaid dresses of red and blue and then each looked her best.

Often coming home from school they would drop in to see Mr. Hall. He kept a basket of McIntosh Red apples on a shelf far from the stove, and when they came he always gave them each an apple and took one himself. The front room of the shop seemed always warm and smelled of bitten apples and white pine smoke, and a little of dust and harness. You could hear the big flies on the windowpanes much more clearly than the automobiles passing along the main street.

"See that ice chest over there?" Mr. Hall might ask. "Electric. When the bank took over the Thompson's place, you never saw such a pile of machinery as they had. Even milked the cows by electricity. I give you my word, I jumped when I saw a common everyday ordinary cat on the doorstep —thought they'd have had an electric rattrap, sure." Mr. Hall chuckled, threw his core into the stove, and lighted his pipe.

"That mantel," he might go on, "came from the big Spooner house up the river. The people who have it now are redecorating it. In the old days, Captain Spooner ordered two carved marble mantels from Italy for the big parlor, but they came on different vessels and the second one was wrecked on Thread of Life Ledges at the mouth of the river in a gale, and he never could get another mantel to match. So now out goes the odd one after fifty years."

"If I were the new people," Alice said, "I'd love to have a mantel whose mate was under the sea being made into coral."

"Well, folks don't all think alike," said old Mr. Hall, "or I'd have nothing to buy or sell. Now here's something curious," and he held toward the children a few big beads in the

69

palm of his hand. "When they tore down the old Palmer place they found these and some more, too, under the hearthstone. They say they were used in trading with the Indians."

It was Marcia who on a coldish afternoon in late October found the powderhorn in a corner with some old cooking things, but it was Alice who loved it on sight. Ten minutes after finding it Marcia had forgotten all about it, but Alice dreamed about it at night. It was made from a cow's horn, closed with wood at the wide end and with a kind of wooden stopper at the point through which the powder had once been poured. The horn had been deeply scratched with all sorts of designs: sunflowers and thistles, fishes, deer, swans, and hearts, and under the date, 1741, was the head of a man in a wig with a lace frill and a crown—the king, of course.

Mr. Hall didn't know much about it. "I bought it with a lot of junk," he said, "but some of the summer people may like it next year."

Alice felt certain that the horn must have come from the old Palmer house where the clapboards had been nailed over square-hewn logs and there were still marks of arrow and bullet holes near the back door. She was sure the horn had been used in the French and Indian wars. Or perhaps it had gone up the Kennebec with Arnold and his men; perhaps it had belonged to the Indian girl Jacataqua who had found the bear which young Aaron Burr shot for the barbecue at Fort Western where Augusta now stands.

Alice thought about the powderhorn a great deal. Then she went to Marcia. "Marcia," she said, "I want to ask you something."

"What is it?" asked Marcia.

Alice swallowed. "Marcia," she said, "do you want that powderhorn at Mr. Hall's?"

"What could I do with it?" asked Marcia, who was practical. "I don't want the old thing."

Then Alice went to Mr. Hall. She found him shingling a chicken coop, for in the fall everyone in Maine shingles something.

"Mr. Hall," she began, trying to speak like her mother, "what are you asking for your powderhorn?"

Mr. Hall looked at her and then took the nails out of his mouth.

"That's a pretty good horn," he said. "I imagine it's worth a basketful of apples, all shined up to look nice and not a wormhole in them."

What a time Alice and Marcia had finding so many perfect apples, even in the big orchard back of Alice's house which the bluebirds loved! Often when they were polishing one that looked perfectly good they would find the smallest speck of a hole and then they would throw that apple out,

71

and race back to the orchard to get some more. At last after a long afternoon's work, they lugged the basket to the junk shop and apparently Mr. Hall was very much pleased. He had the horn wrapped up in newspaper and tied with a red string, waiting for them, and he had another parcel for Marcia, too, which turned out to be four glass balls for a paperweight for her desk.

Alice's father liked the horn almost as much as Alice did.

"Look," he said, "how much yellower it is on one side than the other, where it fitted into the hand while the powder was being poured out. If it could only tell us who had handled it and where it had gone!"

"I think the rainy-day attic would be a good place to keep it," said Alice, which was generous of her, but she wanted her father to share it.

As I said, every year something new is made or shingled or contrived in a good Maine household, and this year Alice's father had been busy taking a part of the big attic next to the stair to make a room where they might all go on rainy days to hear the rain pattering down on the shingles just over their heads. He had Mr. Morse, the carpenter, put in a big dormer window; and Mr. Tibbetts, the plumber, made a hole in the chimney. First they tried a Franklin stove, but that smoked too much, and finally Alice's father came across a little iron stove with a bird on top as a handle and isinglass windows through which you could see the red of the fire, and that did very well.

There was a partition of new boards behind the chimney dividing the new rainy-day attic from the rest of it, and that was the only thing that looked a little out of place with the old brown beams as dark and soft as a moth's wing, and the turkey-red curtains at the windows, with the shelves filled with old books (mostly picture books) and the hooked rugs and the three rocking chairs—"for the big bear, and the middle-sized bear, and the little bear," said Alice—and the cot with the chariot-wheel quilt on it.

But when they brought the horn up, Alice's father had an idea. "Why don't we make a Norwegian sort of room?" he suggested. "We could draw designs from the horn on the new wall and paint them in bright colors and it would be very Northern, and we would do it all ourselves."

It was Alice's mother who drew the designs with a piece of charred wood left in the stove, and it was Alice who painted them with a little help from her father when the work ran too high for her to reach. She had to be very careful not to have too much paint on her brush or the color would drip over the lines and have to be wiped off with a clean cloth.

At the end of four or five afternoons, the wall looked beautiful. There was a sunflower plant on each side of the chimney with heart-shaped leaves and big staring flowers, and

73

two swans facing each other across each sunflower stalk, painted white and outlined with turquoise. In the border, Alice's mother had drawn three hearts.

"Because it's our especial room," she said, and Alice's father added two red apples.

"Because apples were the price of the horn," he said.

Then Alice and Marcia waited for a rainy day. It seemed as though it would never, never come, but at last a morning dawned when the sky was leaden gray and the cold drops began to fall on the bright foliage and the yellowing grass. The little girls raced home from school that afternoon and up the stairs and into the rainy-day attic. Alice's father and mother were already there, popping corn over the stove and pouring it into a yellow kitchen bowl with a big pat of butter on a dish and a salt cellar beside it. There was a great basket of apples, too, and a sweet-smelling bouquet of herbs and the candles lighted. You could hear the rain falling so lightly and steadily on the roof, and the whisper and furling of the flames, and the gay dancing and popping of the corn. There was a little chair waiting for Marcia, too, beside the row of old bound *St. Nicholases*, and the swans and sunflowers and hearts looked down from the wall as though they were happy to have flowered from the old beautiful horn and found a new place in people's lives.

The rain she has a silver broom
A silver broom has she;
She sweeps the flat broad countryside
And house and street and tree.

She sweeps away the blowing dust
Till every leaf is clean,
And tree trunks shine a dripping black
And fields a dazzling green.

Even the dusty sheep which stand
Backs humped against the rain,
Under her broom turn fair and white
Like little lambs again.

VIII

THE BETTER WAY

ONE Saturday morning Alice woke up early. She didn't wake up sleepily to stretch and yawn and stretch again, but sat up wide awake, feeling gay inside. The sun was just rising, too. The grass was silver white with frosty dew, and the reddening leaves of the maple at her window shone and sparkled as though they had been cut from green and ruby glass.

Alice ran down the hall to her father and mother's room and tapped at the door.

"Who is it?" asked her father's voice sleepily.

"It's Alice," called Alice, standing on her toes, "and it's such a bee-eauti-ful day, Daddy!"

"Beautiful enough to get out of bed?" asked her father.

"Yes," said Alice.

"Beautiful enough to get dressed?" asked her father.

"Yes," shouted Alice.

"Beautiful enough to go out?" asked her father.

"Yes!" squealed Alice. How nice it was to have a father

who was always ready to do things just when a child wanted most to do them—and so was Mother.

"Run down and put the kettle on," called Mother, and Alice was downstairs in a flash. She put on the kettle, whipped out the red and white cloth on the table by the east window, set the table for three with the china with the big wreaths of red and blue flowers, and then flashed up the stairs to dress. She started to sing, but roosters in the farms outside the town were crowing and she stopped singing to listen to them. They built towers of bells with their crowing and no two towers were alike. The crowing of the roosters, the glistening of the hoarfrost, the feelings in Alice's heart, were all part of the same thing, something like crystal, something like fountains.

When Alice went downstairs, her mother was already there in her brown dress and burnt-Siena scarf that usually meant woods. There was a smell of coffee and of chocolate, of toast and warm butter. Before you could say Jack Robinson, her father was there, too, and they all had breakfast quickly, talking in whispers so as not to waken Olga.

It was only half-past six when they backed the car out of the garage and took the road. Scarcely anyone was around except a passing truck or two with sleepy-looking drivers who had been at the wheel all night.

"Where are we going?" asked Alice contentedly, but her

77

father only said, "Sh! Somewhere you've never been before."

Birds were sitting on the telegraph wires; a farmer was going into a barn to milk, and a cow lowed as the door swung open. At Nobleboro a cat crossed a green field, stepping high, and farther on a dog ran out barking for pure joy in the morning.

The car turned left on a dirt road, narrow, with deep woods on either side. They passed a clearing with a house in it, and a garden of zinnias and poppies.

"I've been here before," said Alice. "We're near Damariscotta Lake."

"Wait," said her father.

They passed a white farm looking straight down over blue water toward the hills. Cobwebs lay between the heads of Queen Anne's lace, still silver with dew. In the field across the way a fox stood, looking at them like a dog, shining and rosy in the early light. The car plunged down a steep hill into the woods again, and climbed out onto another ridge. Toward the lake was rough pasture, dried sweet fern, pines and sheep among the boulders, hard to tell from the boulders. The car stopped.

But it was not toward the pasture and the blue of the lake that her father led, but away up a little road between two stone walls that Alice had never noticed. After a few minutes' walking through fallen leaves, they saw that they had come to a large open space in the woods. Redtop grass still grew on the slopes, and there were old, unpruned apple trees here and there along the stone walls and a windswept clump of lilacs on a little rise of land.

When Alice saw the lilacs, she knew that a house must have stood near, and sure enough, when they had climbed the wall they came on a little cellar, and a pile of bricks where the old chimney had fallen. Farther on was the well, a round circle of stones with rotten moss-covered boards still laid across it. Alice and her father lifted the boards and they took turns looking down into its dark depths. It seemed like magic to Alice to stare down into that black, round mirror and see far off the blue sky and her own face staring back at her. Perhaps a child who had looked like her had once lived in the lost house. Perhaps a little girl with braids had once dropped her bucket into the well every morning.

Mother must have felt the same way, that the well was rather magic, for she suggested that they should each find a perfect chrysanthemum head and throw it into the well before they covered it up again.

"No," said Alice's father. "Wells like copper. I don't know why. Here's a penny for each of us, and perhaps this is one of the wishing wells that grant one's wishes. At least, it will do no harm to try. Wish, Alice—to yourself, though—and

79

then throw in your penny to the wise old well and perhaps your wish may come true."

So many wishes, but Alice hurried so as not to keep the others waiting.

"May arithmetic be easier this year." She heard a tiny splash. Afterwards she thought she ought to have asked something better than that, something more like the morning and the woods and the wishing well, but that's the way things happen. Someday she'd come back and wish again.

Now they had covered up the mouth of the well and wandered on toward the apple trees.

"Look," said her father, stopping suddenly, "deer have been here."

Then Alice noticed that all through the redtop grass, pale with dew, were narrow strips of darkness where things had been walking, brushing off the drops from the seeded tops as they passed. Under the apple trees the grass was pressed down in three or four places where things had been lying through the night, and some of the apples had been nibbled and dropped.

"See," said Mother, turning to Alice, her eyes shining, "the couch of the deer!"

Alice looked about her; there was not a living thing in sight—only the ruins of the old house, and the half-ruined farm trees, only the encircling woods. Yet here the deer had slept, here they had eaten at dawn when she had wakened in her bed and jumped up to see the early morning.

They followed the tracks to the edge of the woods; by the little stream in the lowlands they saw the small sharp mark of their hoofs, but they caught no glimpse of the deer.

Finally they turned back and Alice climbed into one of the old apple trees. It was unusually hard to get about in it with so many dead branches and so many suckers like thickets, but the apples she picked were delicious, pale yellow with strawberry-color on one side, cool to the touch. They all filled their pockets and walked on down the little wood road.

Now the sun was higher and the earth no longer felt like stone underfoot. They had passed the clearing and were walking through pines, but even among the pines Alice saw old apple trees growing and the round depressions of old cellars.

"There were eleven houses on this road," said Alice's father, "eleven farms. A hundred years ago, this was a well-to-do little community; then as people began to move west, farm after farm was deserted. When I was a boy, there was still one little red house left, over in there," and he pointed toward a hillock overgrown with young pines, "where an old woman lived alone. She was half Indian. People said she could bring sickness on the poultry when she wanted to, and everyone was careful never to anger her in any way, even when she asked for turkey eggs or a piece of calico, or some cornmeal. When the neighbors went to see her, they said there were strange noises all through the house, and doors blew open and shut when there wasn't any wind. After old Aunt Susan died, her little red house fell to pieces like the rest of them, and now there is not a soul even passes on the old road."

"Except us and ghosts," said Alice. "Did you ever see Aunt Susan, Father?"

"Only once," said Alice's father. "I was out hunting partridges and came down the road. There was an old woman in a red wrapper taking a pail of slops to the pig. I remember her hair had not turned gray at all. She stared at me in a queer sort of way."

"Did she say anything, Father?" asked Alice.

"Yes, she said, 'You'll shoot nothing, boy.'"

"And did you?" asked Alice.

"No," said her father with a laugh, "I didn't."

When they could see the high road, they turned back. Their little lost road was not more than a mile long, a forgotten link between two roads still alive. On the way back, they found nothing more but three old headstones, all crooked, in a sumac thicket.

Alice ran across the clearing to stand beside the couch of the deer once more, and then picked a few more apples.

"You'll shoot nothing, boy"

They drove home through a wide-awake world. The sun was shining warm and bright: the hoarfrost was off the ground everywhere, and the trees had lost their sparkle. The usual traffic hummed up and down the roads and in the village people were walking about casually. Olga had cleared away their early breakfast dishes and was baking bread as they came in. The telephone bell rang sharply, and Alice's mother went to answer it with her coat still on.

"That was a good idea of yours, Alice, getting us up this morning," said her father as he put his things away, "but I'm sorry we didn't see the deer."

"Oh, *I'm* not," said Alice earnestly, turning back from the stairs. "Wasn't it really better this way, Father?"

Her father considered the question for a moment, his eyes on Alice's upturned face.

"I do believe you're right, Alice," he said at last, looking at her with an air of surprise and pleasure. "But how did you know that? Very few people do."

"They are gone," said the deer to the doe,
"At the edge of the wood the farm is deserted again.
The horses are gone, and the hound is gone, and the loud
Activity of men.

"They are gone," said the deer to the doe,
"No more is the wind thick with the smoke of their fires,
And the doors are closed and bolted at last, and even the cows
Are gone from their byres.

"They are gone," said the deer to the doe,
"But the orchard is there and the corn
By the edge of the wood. No one will know
When we come with the morn."

IX

THE QUEEN'S CHAIR

MARCIA had grippe and Ellen, Alice's next-best friend, was sick, too. Christmas vacation seemed growing a little long to Alice. Perhaps her mother noticed it, for on the last Friday morning at breakfast she told Alice that she was going over to Wiscasset to see a school friend of hers who was spending the winter there.

"She has twins, two years older than you are," said her mother. "Lucy and Laura, I think their names are, and she suggested that we should bring snowshoes and have a picnic in the woods. She's staying with her sister in the big house that looks down across the river to Edgecomb."

Alice was always a little shy about meeting strangers, but she liked doing things with her mother. There would be the ten-mile drive together, anyway, whatever Laura and Lucy might be like. They stopped at the grocery store and bought two boxes of little sausages and Mother brought one of Olga's fruit cakes wrapped in a damp dishcloth with shamrocks on it.

There had been snow the day before and all the hills were soft-mounded white under a dark gray sky. In some places the drifts on either side of the highway were almost as high as the car windows, and they had the feeling of flying down a tunnel, then again they would come to a clear space and look across white meadows to the dark flow of some river with the woods beyond.

Alice tried not to think too much of what lay ahead. "What are your favorite words, Mother?" she asked.

Her mother swerved from a fallen chunk of ice and answered instantly, "Tranquillity and delight."

Alice thought for a while. "They make me feel the way lilies-of-the-valley do."

Her mother smiled. "What are yours, Alice?" she asked.

Alice considered the matter for a long while, but most of the words that came into her mind were ugly, lumpish words.

"I can't think," she said at last, "but I'll tell you on the way home."

Now they had come to the first bridge where the herons stand in summer, and then through the pines they saw the partly frozen river and the long, long bridge with the town and its churches like a beautiful pattern of roofs and spires on the slope of the hills above the water.

The house where Mrs. Lord was staying was a huge red-brick building with glassed-in porches across its front, looking far down across the old wharves to the river and the houses of Edgecomb across the water. The parlor was oval with high windows draped in long curtains of soft American Beauty color, and smelled of matting.

They had no sooner been admitted by the maid than Mrs. Lord called from upstairs to Alice's mother, begging her to come up while she finished dressing, and just then Miss Craddock, who owned the house, came in to entertain Alice. She was a tall, pleasant woman, with keen gray eyes and an understanding smile. Alice immediately liked her handshake and her low way of speaking.

"Sit down," she said when she had introduced herself. "Oh, you are a wise child. You have chosen the Marie Antoinette chair."

"The Queen's chair?" Alice asked, awed.

"Don't you know about Marie Antoinette and Wiscasset?" Miss Craddock asked. "It was a ship's captain from here who was sent over with his vessel to France during the French Revolution, after the King had been guillotined, to try to save the Queen. While he was getting in touch with her in her prison, he bought up enough of the palace furniture, which the revolutionists were selling, to furnish a house here, so that when she should come to America she might still be among the things she knew and loved. But something went wrong and she did not escape to his vessel, after all. He waited

89

until she was executed and then he returned sadly with all the charming things she was to have used. See, there's the house that was to have been hers."

Miss Craddock stood in the window pointing across the stretch of white and black and silver landscape to a group of houses on the other side of the river.

"That square house above the boathouses was where she was to have lived. It used to be here in Wiscasset, but one winter they moved it across the river on the ice."

Alice looked with both her eyes. The house seemed rather bleak, a white house with a chimney in the middle. She looked down at the little plain painted chair with the cane seat that had once been in a palace, and then sat down in it very carefully.

Miss Craddock smiled at her. "If the captain never brought back a queen," she said, "he did bring back a kind of prince and princess, for it was one of his vessels that carried the first pair of Persian cats to Maine. All the Maine Shags are descended from them. At least, that's what we say in Wiscasset."

Alice could hear footsteps on the stairs. She laid her hands quietly along the smooth wood of the little chair, saying good-by to it. No matter what the rest of the day might be like, she had sat in a queen's chair.

Laura and Lucy came in first, dressed just alike in blue ski suits and looking just alike, too; tall, pale girls with Miss

90

Craddock's eyes and hands. Their mother was little and dark, not at all like them, but nice, too. Alice didn't say much at first, but she soon felt at home, for they immediately began doing delightful things.

"Come on out and help bring Robin to the kitchen door," said Laura, who had thoughtfully put a red handkerchief in her breast pocket so that Alice could tell her from Lucy more quickly at first.

Robin proved to be a very plump, droll donkey with long ears and an innocent babyish expression as well as a will of his own. He had two pack baskets slung on either side of his back, and these the girls packed with picnic things at the back door, while Robin ate snow and waggled his ears. Then they all knelt and strapped on their snowshoes, and the three grown-ups led off and the three girls followed, leading Robin in the path that had been beaten down. At first on the highway it scarcely mattered, but when they came to the wood road, the donkey would have found the going hard if he had been in front. Sometimes, as it was, a hoof broke through and went down deep, but Robin seemed experienced with snow and had the air of thoroughly enjoying himself.

Alice begged to lead him and Lucy gave her the reins.

"Make them as long as you can," she advised. "He can be very mischievous."

"How?" asked Alice, but the twins laughed.

"You'll see," they said, "but it's nothing really bad."

91

Alice walked last. She loved the squeak of the snowshoes on the snow. The bright colors of the others moved ahead through the dark trunks of the pines, over and under the whiteness, and behind her she could feel the comfortable tug of the reins and glance about to see Robin's brown ears wagging contentedly behind her. Then he began to pull harder and harder. She had to haul at him to keep him up with the others. Suddenly the reins slackened and the first thing she knew she was sprawling in a drift, with Robin standing on the long spur of one of her snowshoes.

"He does it on purpose," said the twins, "and then sometimes he hee-haws just as though he were laughing. Do you want us to take him now?"

But Alice still wished to lead Robin.

"I'll go behind, then," said Lucy. "Look, Robin, you bad donkey, you, I'm making a snowball and if you step on any more snowshoes, you'll be sorry."

Perhaps Robin was keeping an eye out for snowballs, as the twins declared; anyway, he walked pretty well back from Alice's snowshoes after that and sent her floundering only once more before they reached the picnic place. In the middle of a grove of spruce trees they found a little roughly built house on runners, with the heavy tongue overgrown with moss.

"It's an old logging shelter," said Miss Craddock, "stand-

"Robin does it on purpose," said the twins

ing just where the oxen last left it ten years ago. Climb up, Alice, slide back the little window up there and you'll find the key hanging on a nail to the right."

Alice had to stand on tiptoe and reach up and feel with blind hands for the key to the padlock. When the door was opened, they found a little stove inside the house. The place was so small that only Miss Craddock went in while the rest brought dry firewood from a shelter near by, or went hunting for garlands of princess pine with which to trim the rough plank walls. Smells of sausages and coffee rose, mixed with the oranges which Mrs. Lord was cutting into a kitchen bowl as she sat on the threshold, still in her snowshoes. Miss Craddock sang "Onward, Christian Soldiers" as she cooked, Robin munched on biscuits, the smoke drifted from the crooked stovepipe with a sweet fragrance, and Alice thought about Marie Antoinette. But she could only imagine her vaguely as she knew her in pictures, with wide silk and taffeta skirts and powdered hair. She couldn't make her seem real and alive in that place.

A dinner bell was ringing from the logging shed on its runners, and everyone was kneeling to unstrap her snowshoes. Within the little building, a plank ran along two sides and another plank let down from the wall for a table, so that six people and the stove could all fit into a space that might be covered by a blanket.

95

"Look out for elbows," said Mrs. Lord. "One, two, three, everyone begin."

It was a merry meal, so merry that the laughter set Robin braying and brought a solitary bluejay to scold at them from a snow-laden bough over the roof of their shelter. No one hurried, the warmth seemed pleasant after the fresh coldness of the outdoors, and when they had finished the last crumb of Olga's cake they sang all the songs they could remember. But at last it was time to scrub out the dishes with snow and repack Robin's panniers.

The way into the woods, which had seemed so long to Alice in the morning, seemed short to her in the afternoon. They were all a little quieter and something of the mystery was gone. Now she knew they were walking toward the town, not toward the heart of the woods. Now things were ending, not beginning.

But one lovely thing happened just under the last big trees. They had all stopped for a moment, and Mrs. Lord walked over to Robin to put her cap into one of his baskets. Just then a load of snow from a bough overhead slipped down and covered her hair with white glistening powder. As she glanced up, smiling, her dark eyes happened to look straight into Alice's, across Robin's back.

For just a moment the picture held, the smiling face under the hair glistening white, the little donkey with red-tasseled

96

bridle, all else in shadow. Then Mrs. Lord patted her hair free from the snow and they all tramped home. But Alice had had her vision. What she had seen and felt for one breath-less second had nothing to do with Mrs. Lord and Laura and Lucy, but went back to the long long ago.

"Have you thought of your words yet, Alice?" asked her mother as they drove home, companionably close, in the early dusk of December.

Alice was not sure. "Mine would be a kind of sentence, not just two nice words like yours," she said. Then she felt a little shy about going on, so spoke quickly: "Do you like 'an exiled queen,' mother, or 'a queen in exile'? 'A queen in exile' has a more solitary sound, don't you think? Like the wind."

Suppose Marie Antoinette *had* come to Wiscasset,
Escaped from Paris, escaped from violence, escaped from fear,
Would she have lived, soberly and quietly
Talking to the women in the square white houses here?

Where they saw gray water, she would have seen steel flashing,
Where they saw autumn leaves, blood she would have seen,
The shivering white birches would have seemed like frightened
    ladies
Where the Wiscasset eyes found only moving green.

And when she saw the women go out into the barnyard,
Then she would have felt her tired heart fail,
Remembering the Trianon and a dress of flowered satin
And herself going milking with a silver milking pail.

X

MISS ABBY OF THE GREEN THUMB

ALICE's mother bought all the eggs for the household from old Miss Abby Stetson.

"Why do you go way down the river when you could get just as good at any of the farms near town?" Alice once heard her father ask.

"I suppose," said her mother thoughtfully, "it's because it gives me an excuse for seeing Miss Abby."

Her father laughed. "Is Miss Abby very exciting?" he said, teasing Mother a little.

"Alice and I think so," said Mother valiantly. "Everything there has grown out of the land: the stones for the cellar were all dragged by oxen from the pastures; the wood was cut from their own pines and taken to the sawmill; and the bricks were made down by the river out of their own earth. She has the molds hanging in the cellar now. And Miss Abby was born in the house and I don't believe has ever been twenty miles away from it in all her life. And when she dies,

99

she'll be buried under the urn monument in the corner of the field, returning to her own Maine dust. It's worth going a few extra miles on a bumpy road to feel the strength of all that."

Alice's father got up from his chair and gave her mother a kiss. Alice had never thought all those things about Miss Abby, but she liked to go with her mother to the old brick house looking down the river, and Marcia always went, too, when she could.

Miss Abby never missed hearing the car drive up—there weren't many cars on the road anymore since the highway was finished. The door would open and there would stand Miss Abby in her gingham dress, waving to them, while a cat or two appeared on the doorsill.

"Come right in," she would say hospitably and begin to lead them toward the parlor, but Alice's mother would ask if they couldn't sit in the kitchen, and there it was they settled down, with the big Clarion wood stove burning warm in the middle, the table in the corner laid for the next meal, and the lovely purple and white Stars of Bethlehem pouring their flowers from their hanging baskets in the sunny windows to mix their blossoms with the geraniums and foliage plants that crowded the window sills.

Miss Abby had the green thumb. She could make every-thing grow. In her dooryard garden, fenced away from the chickens, she had all the old-fashioned flowers and herbs which she called by the old names her grandmother had used: Redcoats and Silver Shillings, Heart's Ease and Comforty Root, Old Man and Old Woman, Bible Leaf and Chiny Asters. She always had little envelopes of seeds to tuck in the egg basket as a surprise, or a cutting which she had been rooting in her window for Alice's mother.

There were always cats under the stove and kittens hiding in and out of the wood pile. Miss Abby kept a jar full of molasses cookies in the big pantry and a jug of milk in the cellarway for little girls. Best of all she had two little white mugs painted with roses and gold leaves. One said, "For a good child" and the other one, "Remember me." Alice's mug was "Remember me." The children were always careful to use their own.

In fall they gathered apples under the high-top apple trees that grew taller than the chimneys. They helped all they could when they were at Miss Abby's—she had so much to do for an old lady. Yet she always pretended not to be busy at all. They never saw her anything but cheerful and smiling until the morning three days after the big February blizzard.

It had been an open winter, unusually mild. Alice and Marcia complained it was hardly winter at all, the snow was so thin and the ice was so bad after the first good snow in

December. Then, just as everyone was beginning to think that winter was nearly over there came a day of thaw; but about midnight people woke up to pull on more covers and the cattle and horses moved restlessly in their stalls. The thermometer had fallen very sharply down, down, down. By morning it was rising again with another shift of the wind and the snow was driving down in a sort of fury.

"No school for you, miss, today," said Alice's father. "I don't want to have to come and take you out from the upper windows."

The blizzard went on for nearly twenty-four hours. Soon there were no cars on the road but the heavy snowplows and their gangs of shovelers, working day and night to keep the highways open. Olga had coffee on the stove all day, and when the snowplow passed she put on a coat and brought the men in for a hot drink and doughnuts which Alice helped serve them. Most of them she knew, neighbors and townspeople, stamping their feet, clapping their hands, and ruefully wiping off their wet, storm-red faces as they stood about joking in the kitchen before giving their thanks and shouldering their way out again into the storm.

Next day the sky was a glorious blue over miles and miles of unbroken, undirtied snow. The landscape seemed so wide and pure; the village was roofed with down.

But it was three days before the river road was broken out.

Alice's mother had tried to reach Miss Abby on the telephone, but the wires were down.

"She's on the farmers' line," said the operator. "You know they put up the poles themselves and they aren't braced to stand a storm like this."

Alice could see that her mother was anxious. Going to and from school, she went every day into the post office to ask if the river road had been plowed out yet. The third day she ran home.

"Mother, Mother!" she called as soon as she opened the front door. "The river road is open!"

In five minutes they were driving carefully along the narrow road with the drifts on each side piled as high as the top of the car. In most places it was like driving through a tunnel, but here and there the walls were lower in a wind-swept place and they could see for miles, across the white hollow where the river lay, past the little farmhouses with their thin plumes of smoke, past forests masked in snow and on, on toward the north pole. The only living thing they saw was a bluejay which flew overhead and lighted in a pine branch at the side of the road, amid a shower of snow, such a strong, fearless-looking bird, with his crest and long tail and his bright coloring and an eye that seemed as boastful as a rooster's.

Later they met another car, which backed a hundred feet

or more to a narrow turnout where it waited while they squeezed slowly past. They were both relieved to see Miss Abby's smoke coming from the chimney. The doorstep had been shoveled out and a narrow path made to the barn—Alice hoped a neighbor had helped. Everything seemed all right, but something, something was different.

For the first time, they had to knock at the door. Miss Abby had not seen them. When she opened the door, she tried to smile at them in the old way.

"Come right in," she said. "I hope you didn't come way out here on my account."

Alice ran ahead into the kitchen. "Why, Miss Abby!" she said. Miss Abby began to cry.

There was not a flower in the room: the Stars of Bethlehem hung shriveled and blackened from their baskets: the very pots were gone from the sills. Trying hard not to cry aloud, Miss Abby led the way into the next room. There by the south window stood a big plantstand in three tiers. It was empty.

"It's all my fault," said Miss Abby. "That night before the blizzard—I never guessed. I let the fire get low." She couldn't help it. Try as she would, a great big sob broke out.

"The worst of it is," she went on, "they were all from my mother's plants, and her mother's before her. It's like losing part of them again."

104

Alice's mother comforted Miss Abby as best she could, while Alice, with a lump in her throat, tried to play with Muffet and Tucker under the stove. But all the way home she was very quiet—absent-minded. The snowy landscape had lost its charm.

"Oh, look!" her mother would cry, but though Alice looked politely, anyone could see that she was scarcely aware of what she was looking at.

"Please *don't* begin daydreaming," her mother said, but Alice scarcely heard her.

When they came into their own big square low house, Alice ran to the plant table and began looking eagerly.

"Didn't Miss Abby give you that, and that, and that?" she asked. "And think how many slips she's sent home to Marcia's mother! And her neighbors. Do you think—"

Her mother clapped her hands. "Why, what good ideas you have!" she said, and still with her coat on, she hurried off to the telephone.

All Saturday afternoon the bell jingled and jangled. Town women came from their living rooms and country women from their kitchens.

"Wait a minute, let me be sure—yes, a lovely Shell Begonia and one of her mother's Surprise Geraniums. . . ."

Sunday morning was as beautiful as Saturday had been. The snowplow had been widening out the river road most of the night. At ten o'clock a row of cars followed each other along it, stopping here and there at farms to pick up well-wrapped passengers. By a little after ten, the cars were drawn close to the left snowbank in front of Miss Abby's and at least fifty people were hurrying toward her door, up the little narrow path, with Alice running ahead, for it had been her idea.

The old lady, shaking with surprise, opened the door, and everyone, smiling and talking at once, came in, men and women and children. It was like a church supper, there was so much jollity, so many queer bundles. Alice's mother gave Alice a little push.

And a bewildered, embarrassed, but happy Alice unwrapped the many folds of newspaper about the bundle in her arms and drew out a white Star of Bethlehem which she handed to Miss Abby.

"It's one of yours," she said. "Not a stranger."

If Miss Abby had cried the day before for sorrow, she cried now again, but this time for joy as everyone began handing her plants.

"You gave it to me five years ago—"

"I raised it from your seeds—"

"It's just bread upon the water coming back to you, Aunt Abby—"

The kitchen window sills were full, the plant stand was

Everyone smiling and talking at once

Everyone smiling and talking at once

overflowing. Blue stars and white stars once more cascaded down from the windows.

Last of all to give her gift was a little old lady, Miss Abby's own age. Her bundle was wrapped up more warmly than any of the others.

"It's the Night-blooming Cereus, Abby," she said. "I wouldn't give it to anyone in the world but you, even if they *had* given it to me first. For it's just about ready to bloom and I was going to invite you all over to sit up with me and watch the first flower come. I've had it nearly ten years and it's never been in blow before."

"Oh, Carrie, you shouldn't," gasped Miss Abby, overcome.

"But I want to, Abby," said the other firmly. "I really want to."

"Then will you all come here?" asked Miss Abby eagerly, raising her voice. "See"—and she pointed to the great bud forming on the narrow thick leaves of the plant in her hands.

"Of course we will," said everyone.

Alice looked at her mother, who looked doubtful. "It may not bloom until two or three in the morning," she said.

"But it may bloom at ten," said Alice's father. "I vote we all come. It won't hurt Alice to be sleepy for a day or two, and the opening of an eight-inch Cereus flower in a room filled with the silence of night and snow outside is a lovely thing to remember."

While some people were unwrapping the flowers, others had been busy with other bundles, and now a voice called out, "Refreshments are ready." Coffee, cream, cake, doughnuts— there they all waited, on Miss Abby's clean red and white checked cloth.

It was a real party: a kind of happiness filled everyone with Miss Abby's happiness. The flowers had come home to the one who loved them best of all. There were more flowers, now, in the house than there had ever been before.

At last it was time to go.

"Thank you, thank you all for my green shower," cried Miss Abby, "thank you all, friends and neighbors."

Alice had a thought that Miss Abby herself looked like a flower brought out of the cold into a warm room, and with that thought she could settle down to enjoy the snow again, and notice what her mother wanted her to see.

Ice shines along the trees and makes
A tinkling music as it breaks,

And soundless footsteps weave a slow
And vinelike pattern in the snow,

By orchard paths where the harsh flute
Of starlings celebrate lost fruit

Frozen, forgotten on the boughs;
Across the hill beyond the house

(A sweep of coldest, purest snows)
The morning sun lies like a rose

Which twilight turns to violet
Against a sky of primrose set.

This frosty garden made of light
Petaled with hillsides smooth and white,

With ice for dew, and for its bees
These hardy birds, can somehow please

The dreaming heart, the quiet eye
More than green June or proud July.

XI

WINTER WEEK END

WINTER comes to Maine with a cold bright severity. The
land is northern and looks its most beautiful with its trees
dark against the endless fields of snow, and its farms wreathed
with balsam banking to keep the floors warm, and little ever-
greens standing by the doors for ornament. The men all go
about in hunters' boots laced to the knees, and almost every-

one wears red jackets that look very gay against the whites and green-blacks of the winter world.

Alice was very fond of tobogganing and skating. There was a hill on the other side of the cove near her house, and as soon as the salt ice had formed she and Marcia often went sliding, sometimes on tin trays just for fun, but more often on their light toboggan. The skating near Damariscotta was not often good because of the salt tides running up and down the great river, but Alice's father sometimes went with them on Saturday afternoons to one or other of the lakes that lay in all the valleys a little back from the coast.

Ellen, Alice's next-to-best friend, spent the summers on a point running out into Damariscotta Pond. Her family had taken an old farm, changing it very little, and sometimes Alice spent the day with Ellen when the haymakers were working in the fields that sloped down to the water, and helped to tread down the hay in the wagon as the men pitched it up from the stubble. She always remembered the heat and the smell of the new hay under her feet and the big rounding clouds that passed overhead all afternoon, and how good the lemonade tasted afterwards under the apple tree.

One Friday morning in February, soon after the blizzard, Ellen came hurrying into the school cloakroom with an air of great excitement.

"Alice! Marcia!" she said to the two, who were getting

113

off their overshoes. "Mother and Father are going up to the farm over the week end. They say I may ask you both if your families will let you come. Father says the ice is simply perfect for skating and we can keep warm with the stoves, and oh, I do hope you may!"

Both Alice's and Marcia's families gave their permissions. The road had been cleared and on Saturday the three children drove to the farm with Ellen's parents. A neighbor had started the fires already, and the farmhouse was beginning to be warm although it had an unlived-in look. Ellen's mother soon had the sheets out airing by the stoves, and Ellen's father brought back a bucket of clear water from the overflow of the springhouse.

"Now," said Ellen's father, "while the grown-ups settle, we thought you children would like to go skating. Here's your lunch and you needn't come back until you hear the bell ringing. Don't go beyond the end of the point, Ellen. There's hot chocolate in the thermos bottle in the little knapsack, so off you go, and have a good time!"

So off the three friends went, running and floundering down the hillslope, Marcia and Alice bright splotches of blue and scarlet, and Ellen a splotch of emerald green on the expanses of the snow. The sky was a soft heavy gray over the treetops, and the wind of the day before had polished the ice clear in great stretches, down which the children skated, laughing and calling out to each other. After about an hour they grew hungry and made their way over to Loon Island, which rose like a ship from the shining surface of the lake, and there they sat on a fallen tree and ate sandwiches and drank hot chocolate.

From where they sat they could see the tracks of little paws in and out of the soft snow lying along the island shore. There was a faint odor of fox on the air, and the children recognized his zigzagging footprints and, more exciting, could make out the unmistakable big track of a moose, which must have passed that way some days before during the thaw, and left his deep mark in slush, now frozen solid.

"Let's leave the things here," said Ellen. "We'll come back for them when Father rings the farm bell for us."

Off they went again, racing down the smooth stretches, hobbling over the rough ones, to fly off again. They never noticed when the sky grew darker and darker and a few snowflakes began to fall. It was not enough to spoil the skating, those few large white flakes falling from the gray sky, and then falling a little faster and faster until they formed a thin fluttering curtain through which the fieldslopes and farms seemed rather strange and distant.

But in the house Ellen's mother looked up and said, "It's begun to snow. Perhaps we'd better call the children in."

And Ellen's father said, "Oh, it's very light yet. We can let them have another fifteen minutes."

By now the children had become aware of the snow and skated faster and faster, trying to pack in as much pleasure as they could in the little while left them. Marcia was perhaps the best skater, but it was she who slipped on a turn and fell, cutting her hand on a piece of ice as she came down. It didn't hurt much, she said, but it was bleeding quite a lot.

"We'd better go in, now, anyway," said Ellen, "and Father will fix up your hand. Oh, dear! I'd forgotten the picnic things. They're still on Loon Island."

Just then the big farm bell began to ring insistently.

"I'll go over and get the picnic things," said Alice promptly. "You take Marcia up, Ellen, and I'll be right along."

"All right," said Ellen, and the two girls skated off slowly, trying to do up Marcia's hand in a handkerchief as they went.

Alice turned away toward the island. It seemed farther off now that she was alone and the snow was falling faster. The bell seemed saying:

"Come quick! Come quick! Come quick!" but she couldn't leave the thermos bottle and things. It looked as though a real storm were coming and they might get buried under the snow. Alice had never been alone on a lake before, but she staunchly kept on. Somehow, she seemed to strike more rough places than she remembered, and made slow time. The snow was certainly falling very fast now and it seemed lonely when the bell stopped its ringing.

She found the picnic things where they had left them, on the fallen tree, and quickly slipped the light knapsack on her back and turned toward home. The snow was falling very fast, but she thought she saw the farmhouse, and even Marcia and Ellen almost at the door.

After that she had to pay attention to her feet: the wind had come up and was blowing loose snow like sand in waving patterns over the ice. She could not see which parts were rough and which were smooth, and the falling snow in her face confused her. When she looked up again, she could not see the farm at all. Perhaps she was too near the shore, now, to be able to see it anyway; she hadn't noticed in the morning. She never noticed things like that and Ellen had been with her then.

A tree was leaning way out over the ice. Surely she would have remembered that! Alice was frightened now, but she told herself not to be silly. In a minute she'd see the path. But was there a real path? She couldn't remember. They had seemed just to run down the slope any which way.

A little farther on she took off her skates and tried to

follow an opening among the trees, but she was soon lost in a thicket, and made her way back to the easier going of the pond. She did not put her skates on again, they were more of a nuisance than a help, but plodded on, her small jaw set. Suppose she should meet a moose now!

"Don't be silly," she told herself. "A moose wouldn't hurt you. Besides, he'd stay in the thick woods on a day like this."

She tried shouting, but she was sure no one would hear her. The few farms were set well back from the lake, often with woods and half-wild pastures between. She felt her heart beating faster at the sound of her own cries and made herself stop.

On and on plodded the little scarlet figure wrapped in swirls of white snow, its footprints wiped out behind it almost as soon as they were made. Now she knew for certain that she was lost.

"I mustn't get into any woods," she told herself. "I must find a real path somewhere, that's all. I must find a real path."

She wouldn't let herself think what might happen if she didn't find a real path, ever: she wouldn't let herself think of her father and mother having tea, now, before the fire in the old house at Damariscotta.

"This is very exciting," she told herself, refusing to sob.

And in the end, she did find a real path. It was narrow, but it lay white among the black bristle of bushes. It led her in its uncertain way over a wall and under a fence, up through a rocky pasture and across a field and right into the kitchen where Mrs. Wincapaw was taking a pan of hot gingerbread out of the oven.

"Why, come right in, dear," said Mrs. Wincapaw. She didn't know Alice, but she was as kind to her as if the child had been her own granddaughter; and soon Alice was sitting with her feet in the oven, eating gingerbread, and telling her story.

Mrs. Wincapaw immediately telephoned Ellen's family. She had to wait for quite a while, but came back satisfied.

"Ellen's father has been looking for you," she said, "but they heard him answer when they rang the bell at the door, and her mother says they'll be over on snowshoes as soon as he gets back. The drifts are blown so bad already she can't get out the car."

Just then Mrs. Wincapaw's big son John came in and ate gingerbread with Alice.

"How'd you like to see the new lambs before you go?" he asked, and Alice said she'd love to. The snow seemed very different with a man beside her, and Prince, the collie, leaping about them and snapping at the soft drifts in his excitement. John pulled back the big red doors of the barn and they walked past the cows which stood in the pleasant twi-light, turning their heads to look at them as they passed.

Alice could see no sheep, but then they came to an incline, leading down below the barn, and there, behind a gate, stood the flock, in a gray underground world walled with stone, lighted only by a small window or two set high above them. The air was cold, but there was no wind and the sheep stood facing the intruders, holding high their heads that looked as though they had been whittled from white wood, and now and again stamping their feet at Prince who barked at them in return.

"Stop that, Prince!" said his master, and the collie stood still, waving his plumy tail, as John walked in among the flock and came back with something in each hand.

"Twins," he said to Alice, "born three days ago," and he put one under each of her arms.

She had never guessed lambs could weigh as little as this: they seemed scarcely heavier than kittens; their skins were much too large for them and hung about them in folds. Under Alice's arms they hung limp with little dangling hoofs, but lifted up their voices in faint baas.

There was an answering baa among the sheep, and the mother ewe thrust her way forward in spite of her timidity, to be near her babies. Alice gave her back her lambs, who ran to their mother unsteadily. The bleating of the flock was a cold sound, like the running of water from melting ice. When they climbed up into the cow barn again and out into the upper world of fields and trees and houses, Alice kept remembering the stone sheepfold under the earth, and the new lambs born below the snow.

"It's like knowing the seeds are coming alive deep down in the ground before any of the leaves are out," Alice told her mother next evening.

She had almost forgotten about having been lost on the pond, and answered her family's anxious questions vaguely.

"I didn't notice much about it," she said at last.

But if Alice forgot some things that didn't interest her, she remembered the things that did harder than most people ever remember anything, and that was perhaps what gave her a certain look in her eyes that made strangers look at her twice. And after that, Alice never went out into falling snow without thinking of the sheep and hearing a faint bleating on the wind.

The stars shine large, the stars shine clear,
The narrow moon is blinding;
The trees make darkness where they stand,
Bright earth to bright sky binding.

When the young laborer brings his pail
Out of the barn's close shelter,
He sees the constellations blaze
In glorious helter-skelter.

The lantern in his other hand
Seems to have lost its light,
So many lanterns hang and shine
And glitter in the night!

XII

A STRING OF SMELTS

ALTHOUGH the cold had been late in coming, it stayed, and in late February the river froze completely except for a hundred feet of dark open water above the bridge where the tide ran so fast in the narrows that the ice could not form even in the coldest weather.

Every morning, Alice on her way to school, stopped on the bridge to watch the wild duck almost below her. Hunger made them tame, and they paid no attention to the human beings above them as they dived in the swift water or rested on the edge of the ice. But the gathering of the ducks soon brought the eagles to perch in the elms along the shore overlooking the rapids, and one morning as Alice and Marcia were standing on the bridge they saw an eagle catch a mallard before their eyes and fly heavily away with it.

Alice could scarcely walk on because of the tears blinding her.

"I hope someone shoots it!" she sobbed.

"Well, I suppose the eagle was hungry, too," said Marcia trying to be reasonable, although she was upset also.

"I hate eagles! I hate, hate, hate them!" said Alice, not trying to be reasonable at all. She felt sad and furious all day at school, and recited her lessons very much at random. At lunch time her sandwiches were filled with her favorite wild-grape jelly, but she ate them with no more pleasure than if they had been made of carrot paste.

When she came to go home she said to Marcia, "I'm *not* going across the bridge."

"What *are* you going to do?" asked Marcia, impressed.

"Go over the ice by the smelt houses," said Alice. "We've never done that. It would be lots of fun, Marcia."

But Marcia shook her head. "I'm going out with Mother," she said. "I've got to hurry. I'll just shut my eyes and run across the bridge."

"You can't shut your eyes and run across the bridge, too," said Alice.

"Yes I can, too," said Marcia. "Or maybe I'll run, or maybe I'll shut my eyes. Anyway I've got to go. You'd better come, too."

"No, I'm going over the ice," said Alice.

Alice had not come to the decision hastily, nor was she one to change her mind hastily either. But it would be lonely and a little scary going without Marcia.

She took a deep breath and turned up the street that led along the river, resolutely turning her eyes away from the trees where the eagles perched. It was a sleepy street of white houses, built mostly by bygone sea captains or shipbuilders. There was no one around, except a cat sitting on a window sill, opening her mouth in a voiceless mew as Alice passed by. Soon the street turned into a road leading to a large empty house on a promontory. The road had not been cleared and the walking was hard, though there was an icy track through the snow made by the smelt fishermen.

Still Alice saw no one, but now the path led past the small graveyard where lay buried the captain's wife who had died of yellow fever far away. Her husband, in spite of the laws, had smuggled her body back, people said, to be laid away in the earth she had known as a girl before she sailed with him to all the ports of the world. She must have been a brave lady, Alice thought. She had once navigated her husband's vessel with only the help of the cabin boy, when all the rest were down with fever and her husband, the captain, lay helpless on the deck and, between bouts of delirium, told her what to do next. A passing vessel had at last answered their distress signal.

Alice wondered what the captain's wife had looked like. It was lonely there, stopping to stare at the weeping willow on the headstone, but Alice felt as though something beautiful were near her. She broke off a little branch of alder berries and a spray of birch catkins, and climbed the stone wall, walking among the few mounds to lay her spray on the old grave, and then went dreamily on among the white birches to the river's edge.

The afternoon sun was halfway down the sky, and there were flowerlike shades of lilac and pale green across the river ice. Before Alice stood what looked to be a village of gnomes, twenty tiny houses, not more than five or six feet square, some colored red and some green, some blue and some brown, but each one with a little stovepipe sticking through the roof, and each pipe with a trail of wood smoke rising from it and vanishing against the sky. Alice knew well enough what they were: in the summer, when the houses were left along the shores of the coves, or back of barns, she had often enough entered their frame and canvas doors; and of course she had seen them in winter, from a distance, in the middle of the ice-covered river, strung along the course of the hidden current, like a little village on a winding road. But this was the first time she had been so near.

Her path lay right among the houses. Standing on tiptoe, she could have touched their eaves. It made her think of Hans and Gretel, and she jumped when someone gave a loud cough near her. She could hear the occasional crack of a stick of wood in a stove, but no one spoke.

Her path lay right among the houses

Then she passed the first open door and, looking inside, saw Mr. Parsons, sitting in an old kitchen chair with a broken back, beside the smallest stove you can imagine, his feet on a board, his elbows on his knees, and his hands holding a line which dropped through a hole in the ice just beyond the rubber toes of his overshoes.

He was a little old man with large careful hands. Alice had often seen him at the post office or on the street and always said good morning, but she had never spoken to him except to thank him for an apple which he had one day unexpectedly pulled out of his pocket and given her.

Somehow old Mr. Parsons must have felt her eyes on him, for he looked up and broke into a smile at seeing her.

"Come in," he said in a hoarse whisper, beckoning with one hand. Perhaps Alice would not have come in, but just at that moment something gave a tug on the line and Mr. Parsons began hurriedly taking it in hand-over-hand, and Alice, caught up in the excitement, came in just in time to see a fine smelt rise head first out of the black hole in the ice and land flapping beside Mr. Parson's chair. The old man chuckled soundlessly, rapped the fish's head on the ice and let down his line again. No sooner was it in the water than he was pulling it up again, with an even larger and fatter fish on it. Mr. Parsons disposed of it, and then paused to put a small piece of wood in the small stove.

"Like to try?" he whispered rustily again, and moved over to give Alice half the chair.

Alice didn't quite know whether or not she wanted to try, but it would be exciting to be able to tell Marcia that she had really caught a fish, and so she sat down, put her feet on the board, too, and while Mr. Parsons lighted his pipe that he had let go out, dropped the line into the mystery of the dark river rushing under them, where the fish lived in a winter night without sun.

For a long time nothing happened. Alice's tenseness changed to restlessness. And she looked about her. The tiny canvas house was warm and snug. There was a little pile of wood, a market basket filled with fish and two or three hazel twigs. In one corner hung a small mirror. Alice couldn't imagine why. Just when she was wondering what she would say to Mr. Parsons about having to go home now, the line gave a great jerk between her hands. It felt as though a whale had hold of the other end.

"Haul it in! Haul it in!" whispered Mr. Parsons, and Alice began to haul. Looking into that black hole she thought that anything might come out of it; she felt almost afraid to see what she was hauling to the surface. But when at last it was drawn up flapping, it proved to be quite a small smelt. Mr. Parsons killed it quickly and again Alice dropped her line.

An hour later she had forgotten everything except the excitement of dropping her line into the unknown, and it was Mr. Parsons who at last whispered it was getting late and maybe her ma'd be worried if she didn't get home soon.

"Here, you mustn't leave without your first fish!" he went on. "Wait while I string them for you," and he hooked a dozen of the dead fish through their gills on an alder shoot and handed the end to Alice.

"You caught them all," he said. "Tell your ma that and ask her if you can't come to see my wife and me some day. We never had a little girl of our own, you tell your ma. You'd like my workshop. Of course I don't do big carvings anymore, but I putter round still. You'd like it, I know."

And Mr. Parsons looked at her eagerly. Alice laid her hand on his knee.

"Of course Mother will let me come. She says you're the last of the figurehead makers—oh, perhaps I oughtn't to say that!" Alice stopped, confused. It sounded so sad to tell someone that he was the "last" of anything.

But Mr. Parsons didn't seem sad. "Far as I know I am," he whispered cheerfully. "There was a lot of us in the old days, but I figure since Jem Day down to Bath went, I'm the last of 'em," and Alice could see he felt proud to have outlived them all.

"I'm sure I can come," she whispered again.

131

Someone from the next house went "shh!" So much talk might disturb the fish.

Alice tiptoed back and put her mouth almost to Mr. Parson's ear. "May I come here again?" she asked.

"Wind's turned southwest," he said. "We'll see."

The sun was very low as Alice crossed to the other shore. Ice and snow, and trees and the village beyond lay all in shadow, but the sky was still bright with light and the cock on the steeple near her house glittered fiercely above the shadowed streets. Her branch of fish weighed heavily, but she was very proud of them. They *were* beautiful, too, even without the sunshine on the dark rainbows of their backs. Everyone spoke to her about them, and her mother was very much surprised.

"We'll have dinner a little late, and Olga will roll them in flour and bake them," said her mother. "Alice, what an exciting thing to have happen on a perfectly ordinary day! They look delicious."

And they were as delicious as they looked, tender and sweet. Alice felt very proud of her fish that she had caught herself and brought home from the mystery of the hidden waters. It was only as she was undressing that she suddenly thought, "Why, I'm no better than the eagle."

Then she thought some more and said to herself, "Or maybe the eagle isn't any worse than I am."

But though she no longer hated the eagles, she was glad next day that the thaw had set in and soon water was appearing in a dozen places. The ducks scattered to safer fishing grounds and Alice could cross the bridge again with a light heart.

Who knows what's moving under the ice?
Who knows what's moving along with the tide?
Dark flows the river hidden from sight,
Its currents are cold and swift and wide.

Its currents are cold and swift and wide,
Under the ice it darkly flows,
But what is moving there with the tides,
What life lies hidden—who knows? who knows?

XIII

THE LAST OF THE FIGUREHEAD MAKERS

BY THE end of March, Maine was deep in mudtime. Most of the snow was gone: there could be no winter sports, and the thawing ground was dark and soggy to look at. Every lawn had turned into a bog and the country roads were almost impassable.

"I looked down one of those ruts on the mill road," said Alice's father, "and really I expected to see the roof of a pagoda down there."

Yet spring was in the air, water was running everywhere, and the first brave flowers were appearing on the south sides of houses and the first brave songbirds returning. Alice wanted to do something, but there didn't seem much to do— at least nothing different. She was tired of her winter clothes, but it was too early to wear spring dresses; she was tired of school; she was even tired of books.

"What shall I *do* this afternoon?" she began asking her mother, but to everything her mother could suggest, she said unhappily, "Oh, I've done that hundreds of times."

Then one afternoon Alice met Mr. Parsons coming out of the barbershop, and they stopped to speak.

"Coming round to see my workroom some day?" the old man asked shyly.

"I'll come right now if you're going home," said Alice.

Long ago, on the afternoon when she brought back the smelts, she had asked her mother if she might go there, but the idea had slipped her mind. Now she wondered why she had forgotten it. Mr. Parsons was so glad that she was coming. He pointed out the places where the shipyards used to be when he was a boy.

"You could hear the sound of the men's hammers from dawn to dark in Damariscotta in those days," he said. "Our vessels went everywhere, of course: the West Indies and China and Africa, too, but the most of them went along the

136

coast carrying bricks from the brickyards down the river. Bricks, ice, and lumber: yes, and herring in the spring: that's what Damariscotta exported."

"Where did the ice go to?" asked Alice. It was hard to think of anyone shipping ice—it was such a common thing.

"Most of our trade was with the West Indies," said Mr. Parsons. "Those people down there would pay anything, within reason and out, for ice. They'd never had a sherbet or a cool drink in their lives until the Yankees began packing ice in sawdust and sending it to all the hot places on the globe. We had sawdust enough in those days, with all the lumber being cut and vessels, too, and nearly every farm bordered on a pond. Most all the farmers got their ready money in winter by cutting and hauling ice to the icehouses on the rivers. I had a cousin was a blacksmith and made a good living just shoeing the horses required for the work. Times have changed a lot."

Mr. Parsons shook his head, but he didn't look at all gloomy. Now they had come to the little road that led up to three or four houses hidden by trees from the broad swirl of the river below them. A board walk kept people who were walking out of the mud and the little road had an old-fashioned look very different from the highway so near it with its endless passing of trucks and cars.

Mr. Parsons' house was painted yellow with white trimmings. The front door and the back door each had trellises, carved, with grapevines over them. At the top of the front-door trellis was an eagle with wings spread out, and at the top of the back-door trellis was the head of a woman with flowing hair. A large seal of the State of Maine hung between two windows and on the roof was a little cupola of glass, set in a design of carved sunflowers.

The house faced to the south and was as cheerful looking as a house could be and just seemed to fit Mr. Parsons. Inside it was just right, too. The floors were covered with carpets right to the walls, and the papers were brown with gold patterns. All the picture frames were carved, and there were hanging shelves covered with wooden flowers of all sorts. A ship's model in a glass case stood on a table between the front windows, and there were photographs of figureheads Mr. Parsons had carved, and embroidered pictures from Japan where Mr. Parsons' brother had sailed as a young man.

Mrs. Parsons was little and old and kind, too, and she gave Alice caraway-seed cookies and played "Abide with Me" on the organ, letting out the stop which made bells peal with every note. Alice had never heard anything like it. She tiptoed about asking questions and feeling as though she had come into a storybook.

But best of all she liked the workshop in the shed. It was

a little room with a stove in it and the smell of shavings. Mr. Parsons was making a sign for the fire station, with a hook and ladder and an ax and a fireman's hat on it in relief. It was almost finished and Alice sat on a stool watching his big bony hands so sure and certain, peeling away thin curls or cutting downward into the wood.

"It looks such fun," said Alice softly.

"You must try your hand at it, too," said Mr. Parsons. "What will you make?"

"I couldn't make anything," said Alice.

"Anyone who wants to can make *something*," said Mr. Parsons, and as he went on working they talked over things that she might do. Mother's birthday was in a little over two weeks. It might be something for her. And after a little Alice thought of Mother's four-poster bed with its hangings. It always seemed to her that there ought to be something on top of the posts, above the canopy, and Father said there were holes as though something had fitted in once.

"Probably they took the tops off when the bed was in a low-ceilinged chamber, and they got lost," said Mr. Parsons. "There might have been eagles, but they would be too hard for you, of course. Pineapples are easier. And then there are flames."

After talking about it, they decided on flames. Mr. Parsons took a carpenter's pencil and made a drawing of the kind of flame he meant, like a candleflame bent in the middle a little by the wind.

"It looks better to make it look like two tongues of fire joined," he said. "It's not hard. I'll help you."

They chose the wood together, an old piece of pine, and Mr. Parsons sawed it for Alice into four blocks and fastened the first one into the vise and showed her how to mark the wood and then begin cutting it down. On the first flame he helped her a good deal, but by the time she reached the second flame she knew pretty well what to do and only came to him at the hardest places. Every afternoon she could scarcely wait for school to be out to hurry off to Mr. Parson's workshop. She was very mysterious about it all and wouldn't tell even Marcia what she was doing. Mudtime was forgotten. Rain only meant to her now that the light would be bad. Once she cut her hand a little, but Mr. Parsons neatly bandaged it for her and she went right on working.

"You have a good touch," he told her. "You have a feeling for wood."

When it grew too dark to work she lingered a little, while Mr. Parsons told her the stories of the ships which had sailed away with the figureheads of the large ladies in old-fashioned basques and billowing skirts whose photographs were on his walls.

"That was the *Belle of Bath*," he would explain. "She was in the China trade for years and then was lost on the return passage in a gale off the Isles of Shoals. That one was for the *La Reine Marie* which sailed from Thomaston. Eliphalet Day was her master: I remember Mrs. Day sailed with him alternate voyages. She thought she should spend half her time with her children ashore. I think the *Marie* was sold for the coal trade in the end, but I never heard what happened to her. That was the *Endurance*. They leased her to a company in the West Indies. That dolphin and scroll was for one of the little vessels that ran out of Round Pond to the African Gold Coast. Funny thing to think of a village like that shipping to Africa! When I was a young man, hardly a family in Round Pond didn't have a monkey and parrots for the children. Yes, and carved elephant tusks in the parlor."

The story Alice liked to hear best was of the Damariscotta witch who kept a boarding house for sailors and heard the Damariscotta captain and the Rockland captain arguing as to which one had the better vessel.

"She was full of pride in her town," Mr. Parsons would go on, "so she called the Damariscotta captain into the hall.

" 'I'll prove how fast your vessel is!' she said to him. 'You go aboard now and break out her sails and I'll blow and I'll blow and I'll blow you a wind, and you'll be in Boston by morning.' "

Then Mr. Parsons would have to blow his nose.

"Go on, go on," Alice would demand even after she knew the end of the story, and Mr. Parsons would clear his throat.

"So the captain gave her one look and then he went aboard. It was midnight but he routed out the crew. They had a following wind down the river and when they reached the sea it veered to the northeast and freshened. Yes, a regular gale, straight behind them all the way. The men said afterwards it was like flying. And they were in Boston by morning."

"Did you make her figurehead?" asked Alice the first time she heard the story.

"No, she was built before my time," answered Mr. Parsons, fumbling in the corner where various blocks and boards lay, and returning with a banister from a rail which he put in Alice's hand, "but here's something I picked up when they were breaking her up at the yards. There's a bit of pine that's been bewitched, if you believe the stories people tell."

Only one thing happened to dim Alice's pleasure in wood carving. A week before her mother's birthday it became clear that she would never be able to finish all four finials.

"Suppose I make the other one for you? I've no orders just now," said Mr. Parsons, peering at Alice kindly.

Alice had a vision of what Mr. Parsons' flame would look

142

like. Her three on which she had worked so hard would seem crude and clumsy by comparison. But she wouldn't spoil Mother's present by wanting her work to seem better than it was.

"Oh, thank you, Mr. Parsons," she said, with scarcely any pause at all.

"We'll wait until we see if you can't finish them yourself," went on Mr. Parsons.

But though Alice worked as fast as she could there were only three flames ready on the afternoon before her mother's birthday.

"I'll do the other one tonight and have them wrapped up for you to take home tomorrow when you come from school," said Mr. Parsons.

The next afternoon Alice carried back the four finials in a big cardboard box. She had bought a birthday card to go with them, but she felt a little sober as she put them in her mother's lap and kissed her.

Her mother was exclaiming with surprise as she took out the first finial. It was one of Alice's. Her mother thought it was beautiful.

"Why, Alice!" she said. "My bed will look twice as lovely now!—and to think that you made them yourself, dear!"

"Mr. Parsons helped me some," said Alice, but she couldn't help feeling very proud until she remembered.

"One of them he made himself, because I couldn't do it in time."

Wait until Mother saw Mr. Parsons' flame! She wouldn't think much of Alice's then. But the next one was hers, and so was the next, and the fourth one was surely hers. There was the place where she had cut in a little too deeply on one side. She couldn't believe her eyes. Which one was Mr. Parsons'?

"I think they're all stunning," said Alice's mother.

Alice stood flooded with happiness. Mr. Parsons hadn't shamed her. He had understood and turned his adept hand for once back to a beginner's for her sake.

"Oh, Mother!" Alice cried, her brown eyes shining. "Mr. Parsons is the nicest man in the world—next to Daddy."

Spring is too busy to dress just now,
　　Busy with buds, inexperienced bees,
Busy with lambs and ducklings and trees,
　　Busy with nests at the end of the bough—
　　Spring is too busy to dress just now!

But wait till the time of beginnings is over,
　　Wait till her little weak things are secure,
She'll dust off the mud on her dresses, be sure,
　　And pluck for her throat both lilacs and clover—
　　Spring will be lovely when hard work is over!

XIV

VINEGAR TOM

"Suppose," said Alice's father one evening, "you ask Marcia if her father and mother will let her come to Monhegan with us. We'd go on Thursday and come back on Saturday. You've never been on one of the outer islands, and there's nothing like them."

Alice was so happy that she almost—yes, really and truly —almost forgot to tell Marcia at all. But she did tell her in time, and early Thursday morning the two little girls were in the rear seat of the car, waving to everyone they knew as they drove out of Damariscotta headed north.

There were the Indian shell heaps, and then came the monument to Captain Noble who fought in the colonial wars; there lay Waldoboro on its steep hill above the river, like a Jacob's ladder of neat red and white buildings; now came the woods and the distant views of the Camdens, like real enchanted mountains; and last, here was the long common of Thomaston.

A man from one of the garages drove down with them to the end of the wharf, past old forsaken warehouses that looked like huge jails, and then they were piling out and in no time at all they were on board the *Nereid*, which was built like one of the local fishing and lobster boats, but larger and stronger, to carry mail and supplies through ice floes and storms to the people on Monhegan.

The first ten miles lay down the St. George River; and the children ran about the narrow deck, and into the pilot house, and down into the small cabin, examining the cargo of milk bottles, groceries, and a crated sewing machine, calling out as flocks of duck flew past the *Nereid's* bows, or staring at the cormorants perched dark and ungainly on the buoys that marked the passage.

But when the *Nereid* headed for the sea, something seemed different.

"Do you feel a little queer, Marcia?" Alice asked.

"No," said Marcia, "but Alice, you look awfully funny— Oh, look, that must be Burnt Island and see all the sheep!"

"I don't care about sheep," said Alice in a small voice.

"It's always pretty pickety here," remarked one of the men who happened to be going by, but it was just as bad when they left Burnt Island.

"Oh, look at the porpoises!" cried Marcia.

But Alice wouldn't have been interested even in whales

147

just then. Her mother came and sat down on the deck with her back against the pilot house, and Alice lay with her head in her mother's lap, all wrapped up in a steamer rug. She shut her eyes and wondered how Indians had ever come here, away out in the ocean, in their canoes to fish; she wondered about the sailors from England and France who had crossed from Europe in their little fishing boats and dried their cod on these island beaches before Maine was even explored. Then she pretended that she was one of the early settlers escaping for safety from the shore. If she opened her eyes, she would see the smoke of the burning cabins rising above the dark trees. The Indians were angry and meant to wipe out the white people from their land; how lucky her family was to have taken to the shallop in time! There were other boats in the distance, a rowboat from somewhere and a pink from Damariscove Island with a cow in it—she could hear it mooing—and some of the people from New Harbor had escaped in canoes. Alice was imagining so hard that she forgot and opened her eyes and then shut them with a sigh.

"Feeling better?" asked her mother, leaning over her.

Alice with her eyes screwed tight shook her head. "Worse," she whispered sadly.

But even an hour and a half must pass in time. Marcia's feet came racing down the deck.

"Look, look!" she shouted. "We're almost there!"

148

Then Alice raised her head. Before them lay an island with spruces sloping up to hills and cliffs. There were square scattered buildings below a lighthouse facing a narrow channel of water which separated Monhegan from a small rocky island. This was the only harbor, where lay the fishing boats, rising and falling to the swells, while the sea gulls cried above them. Before she knew it, Alice was on the wharf, very glad to be on solid land. Then she looked about her. The air had a wild sweet smell as though no one had ever breathed it before; there had been rain the day before and all the cliffs shone in the spring sunlight like silver; the waves came shouldering in from the sea, sending up great spurts and fountains of spray against the rocks, and overhead the crying gulls shone blindingly white. Somehow the people on the wharf went with the scene. They had a free, masterful air, even the children.

"Father, it's noble!" cried Alice skipping.

Her father looked down at her: round face, clear eyes, brown pigtails—he would not have changed her for any other child in the world.

"Yes, it's noble," he said. "You didn't mind being sick?"

"That wasn't anything to pay for all *this*!" said Alice.

The house in which they stayed looked straight over the harbor, across to the great rocky humps of Manana. There were always cats on the kitchen doorstep and seagulls some-

149

where in the air, and it was sometimes hard to tell which were mewing, gulls or cats. The house belonged to an old fisherman who still wore rubber boots almost up to his waist, though he was over eighty years old, and sat most of the time in the rocking chair beyond the stove. It was his daughter who kept house, had everything spotlessly clean, made the best chowders and pies, and found plenty of time to play the parlor organ and sing "Throw Out the Life Line" and other nautical hymns.

As soon as lunch was over, they went walking on the outer cliffs. Not a house, not a person was in view; only a little path led in and out, up and down over great rocky headlands, in and out past inlets and chasms. Marcia went first, then Alice, with Mother behind her to see that she didn't step off the path into the sea while being absent-minded, and last of all came Father to keep an eye on everything.

Here on the island all the snow was gone: there was a delicious odor of wet earth which mixed with the odor of the sea. The waves came rolling in from the bright ocean, and the island cliffs seemed to lean forward to meet the on-coming sea; crash, crash, crash, roller after roller struck the cliffs and broke, the torn water flung high into the air. It seemed like the beginning of the world. "Chaos and old Night," Father said, and when they were a little overawed by so much might and beauty, their path would lead into small meadows where the trailing yew made dry green rugs for the children to lie on, a few inches above the wet spring ground.

All afternoon they scrambled up and down paths and hung above precipices and shouted into the wind, and it was nearly sunset before they turned home. As they were passing by Gull Rock, a great slab of granite and feldspar thrust out against the breakers, Alice thought she saw something.

"Look!" she said.

"Where?" asked Marcia. "I don't see anything."

Alice pointed.

"Yes, something *is* moving on the very top of Gull Rock," said her mother, who had good eyes.

"It isn't a gull," said her father. "It's some sort of animal, but why in the world would an animal be way out there in the midst of the surf?"

"It's a cat," said Alice.

As they drew nearer, they saw that it was indeed a cat, sitting on the topmost peak of the rock gazing quietly out over the tumble of lavender and rose-colored sea. It looked very small there against the whole ocean, but there was nothing of fear in its calm pose. Woods behind it, the entire ocean under its paws, it sat thirty feet above the thunder of the breakers, in the strange light of the sunset, as though lost in thought.

151

"Kitty, kitty, kitty!" called Alice from the path. "Come, puss, puss! Come, kitty, kitty, kitty!"

The cat turned its head, slowly rose, stretched, and came down an almost perpendicular slide of rock, picked its way through a sort of valley, and going neither fast nor slow, joined the human beings waiting above on the path.

"It's an old tom," said Alice's father. "See his big round head with all the scars on it."

"He's thin," said her mother. "I believe he has gone wild and lives in the woods."

The cat gazed indifferently out to sea while they talked, but when they began to walk he walked with them, sometimes ahead of Marcia, sometimes as rear guard.

He was a yellow cat with stripes through the yellow and his coat was very thick. His eyes were almost the same color as his coat. When anyone said, "Kitty," he stared at the speaker, looking straight into his eyes, as few animals ever do.

"He seems like a power," said Alice's mother, "not like a cat."

"He's a witch's cat," said Alice. "And I'm—"

"And you're what?" asked her mother.

"Oh, nothing," said Alice. "Do you think he'll come back to the cottage with us?"

"It must be half a mile from here," said her father. "I don't suppose he'll follow long. If he's a witch cat, I think his name is Vinegar Tom, for that was the real name of a real witch's cat once. But we'd better hurry. It's getting dark."

And hurry they did and Vinegar Tom slipped along in the dusk with them. When they reached the door, there he was sitting, gaunt and impassive, on the doorsill.

"Oh, now we can give him something to eat," cried Marcia rushing indoors. The grown-ups went in, too, but Alice sat down beside Vinegar Tom without trying to touch him and waited till Marcia came out with a fish head and a saucer of scraps.

"Miss Sears says the island is full of cats," said Marcia. "There's not a horse or cow, or pig or chicken, or fox or deer on it, she says, and even the sheep are gone, but there are a few dogs and lots and lots of cats to keep the rats out of the fish houses. Half of them are wild, she says, and she's heard people say that there's one that sits on Gull Rock every evening at sunset time, no one knows why, but she hasn't ever seen him before."

Darkness had come on and the great beam of the lighthouse lantern, high above the village, slowly swept the sky and then slowly brushed through the settlement; it shone in the eyes of the children and was gone. It was cold now, and strange. There was no sound but the continuous low growl of the sea gnawing at the rock. Vinegar Tom had finished the last scrap of food and now solemnly stared ahead of him, not turning his head from the passing brightness of the light when it shone into his eyes.

"Come in, children," called Alice's mother from the door. "It's getting too cold out there."

Just as she turned to go in, Alice brushed her hand against Vinegar Tom's scarred head and for the first time heard his voice raised in a rusty purr.

Her first thought when she woke in the morning was to know if Vinegar Tom were still there. She looked out of the window. He was sitting in the sun, staring out to sea, paying no attention to Miss Sears' cats who eyed him suspiciously from the doorstep. As Alice watched, Miss Sears opened the door, and shook a dishcloth.

"Scat!" she called. "Scat!"

Alice ran down the stairs, without waiting to braid her hair.

"Oh, please, please! Miss Sears," she begged, catching the astonished woman's arm, "don't drive Vinegar Tom away."

"I've seven cats of my own," said Miss Sears. "I can't feed all the cats on the island."

"But I *think* this is going to be my cat," said Alice.

"Gracious, child," said Miss Sears, "you don't want *that* old thing. I can let you have one of my white angora kittens and welcome. And there's the prettiest family of short-tailed

"Scat!" she called. "Scat!"

"Scott," she called, "Scott!"

cats over at Mrs. Trefetheren's. I'm sure she'd be glad to let you have your pick of them."

"Marcia can take a kitten," said Alice. "The only one I want is Vinegar Tom."

"Well, then, I won't chase him away," said Miss Sears. "Here's some turnip peelings he'll like. I can't let you have any milk, for that has to come from the Main, you know. Then you'd better get your hair done, for breakfast is just about ready."

Vinegar Tom purred again, a single rusty purr, when she came near him, and after breakfast he followed them all to the fish houses and the shore, and sat indifferently on top of a lobster pot while they talked to the fishermen. When they rowed over to Manana Island to see the Norse runes near the foghorn station, he was still on the lobster pot and an hour later he was there to meet them on their return. In the afternoon he went up to the lighthouse with them, paying no attention to anyone except for the single purr he gave whenever Alice spoke to him.

They met many cats, on the beach by the fish houses, on the walks and doorsteps, cats of all ages and of all kinds. But Alice had no eye for any of them. She looked troubled. That night at supper she poured milk into her water glass half full of water, tried to use her fork for a soup spoon, and said, "Yes, Mother," whenever anyone, even Miss Sears, spoke to her.

"What *is* the matter, Alice?" asked her mother at last, but Alice didn't hear. "Alice, what *is* the matter, dear?" she repeated.

"Nothing," said Alice, putting much too much salt on her fish.

"It's that yellow tom," said Miss Sears, stopping in the doorway with the platter in her hands. "The child's set her heart on that half-starved old cat."

There was a pause. Mother looked at Father; she was thinking of how she had always refused to have a cat because of the birds, but somehow this seemed different.

"He could have a bell . . . and stay in nights . . ." she murmured uncertainly. They nodded at each other.

"All right, dear . . . if you'll remember to feed him," Alice's mother said.

"I'll never forget," cried Alice, leaping up to kiss everyone. She ran to the door. There, faintly, she saw a little way off Vinegar Tom, sitting and staring at the new moon. The tide had turned, and the breakers sounded louder in the night air. Overhead the beam of the lighthouse lantern solemnly circled the darkness.

Alice could have found no words for all that she felt.

She ran to Vinegar Tom and laid her fingertips on his scarred head. "I'm going to be your witch," she said.

Vinegar Tom gave his short sudden purr.

They have never seen a meat cart,
They have seldom tasted meat,
But fish is what they dream of
When they dream of things to eat,
And when their master's dory
Comes rasping up the shore
The cats and kits run thronging
To share the fish once more.

They have seldom seen a robin
Nor a sparrow flying by,
But before their eyes were opened
They knew well the seagull's cry,
They knew well the seagull's mewing
And the sea's unending beat
And their master's step, home coming
With sea boots upon his feet.

They have never heard of cat shows,
But their hair is long and soft,
And their tails are plumed and shining
And they carry them aloft
As they hurry down politely
(But not greedily at all)
To congratulate their master
On the flavor of his haul.

XV

TO SEE THE HERRING RUN

THE eagles had come back to the river. Alice had not seen them near the bridge since February when the first thaws came and the duck scattered, but now it was May and here they were wheeling against the blue sky, their tails and heads making specks of dazzling white in the sunlight. All the children knew what that meant.

"The herring are running," Alice told her father and mother at supper.

"I thought they would be, soon, with this warm spell," said her father.

"Tomorrow afternoon we'll go out and dig dandelion greens, Alice," said her mother.

Alice didn't like either herring or dandelion greens very much, and yet that rather disagreeable meal always seemed the beginning of the real spring. There were two springs, one of mud and pussywillows and running ice water, and a second spring when even the leaves looked like flowers and in all the branches one saw birds with throbbing throats, and there were a great many turtles crossing the roads. Herring and dandelion greens were connected in Alice's mind with that lovely spring, and with coats left hanging in closets.

"Goodee!" she said. "I know where a lot of dandelions are coming up back of the orchard. I'll come right home from school and Marcia can dig them for her mother, too."

That was what the herring run had always meant to Alice; eating them as a sort of movable spring feast, like turkey for Thanksgiving. She got out her books after dinner to study, but studying was very hard. In the fall everything about school had seemed very exciting, but now even the smell of the books was dull and dreary. She kept wishing that she had lived in the days of King Arthur when ladies weren't expected to study, but to sit on chairs hung with velvet and crown their victorious knights with wreaths of roses. Arithmetic was the worst. No lady in the old days was expected to know anything about arithmetic. Alice had done one problem five times and it was as wrong as ever.

"I just can't do it," she said aloud. "I've tried and tried and it doesn't come out."

"Try it in the morning," said her father. "You'll be fresher then."

Alice went to bed, glad to be rid of homework. No one expected her to lie in bed thinking of arithmetic, but she could imagine knights cantering great horses down forest paths, and girls with wands of willow herding their geese in small green meadows. Her room filled with white light—the moon must be rising. She heard a few birds twitter and then fell asleep.

It was unusual for Alice to wake up once she had fallen asleep, and unheard of for anyone to waken her. Yet now she was waking, with her mother's hand on her shoulder.

"What is it?" she asked sleepily. "What do you want, Mother?"

"There is the most beautiful moon outside you ever saw," said her mother. "It's nearly as light as day and Daddy and I are going up to the Mills to see the herring run. We thought it was an occasion and that you might like to come, too."

Alice's mother spoke a little hesitatingly. Alice had looked so sound asleep, her hair streaming over her pillow. But if

Alice's mother had doubts, Alice had none. She was out of bed and into her clothes in a moment, half-asleep as she was. Outside it was cool and silver. The moon was full and there were no clouds, and not many stars, but a white light flooded all the world, washing across the meadows, twinkling among the trees, making the white houses seem cut out of marble.

They all sat in the front seat of the car, Alice in the middle, and no one said anything at all. The Mills were only three miles away: there were no mills anymore, but the town was still called that, and the water still came tumbling down the cascades from the lake above to the tidewater river that lay below. People who lived at the Mills must always hear the sound of falling water in their ears, and see the flicker of reflected light on their kitchen ceilings. They were probably so used to it that they scarcely noticed at all. But Alice noticed.

First they walked beside the long fish sheds on a wharf which was slippery with scales. All along the walls stood new barrels, some empty and some filled with fish, and there was a strong damp under-the-sea sort of smell, everywhere: a sad sort of smell, Alice thought to herself. The water beside them was packed with fish, swimming upstream. At first, Alice did not notice them: they looked like a heavy shadow, but there they were, herring, body pressed close to body, blue-black back next to blue-black back, just below the surface for as far as she could see, and all of them headed up-stream and moving like a carpet slowly being dragged along. Sometimes the backs of some of the herring came above the water, like ripples going the wrong way. Sometimes one fish turned on its side and there was a sudden gleam like moon-light in the darkness.

A small walk with a rail led to where the two halves of the stream united. On the left, the water came down into a large basin from a real fall that no fish in all the sea could have leaped: on the right, the stream came down a series of cas-cades, made into small basins edged by fieldstones. When the fish came to the two down-pouring currents, some went blindly to the left, some went blindly to the right.

The fish that swam to the left filled the large basin at the bottom of the falls and were trapped there, as they never turned back.

"You see the chute overhead?" Alice's father asked. "Dur-ing the day the men shovel them up into the chute, which slides them right down to the packing house, where they barrel them for the West Indies, except for those which every householder at the Mills can demand free and the ones that other people buy. But most of them are shipped away to be eaten by the negroes."

"What happens to the ones that go to the right?" asked Alice.

"Oh, they are protected," said her father. "No one can touch those. They go and spawn in Damariscotta Pond, and later the young fish go to the sea. But they never forget the pond where they were born and they will come back thousands of miles to that same place and no other to spawn when they are grown."

Alice sighed. The fish on the right were safe. She looked down at the ones to the left, a vague dark mass in the moonlight pointing their silly noses to falls they couldn't climb.

"If I had ever done a fairy a favor, I'd ask her to turn me into a herring." She thought a little. "I'd want, of course, to be very, very sure that I could turn back again as soon as I needed to. Flap my tail three times out of the water, or something."

Again Alice brooded, leaning against the rail. She was telling herself a story as she often did.

"I'd talk to them in fish language and tell them, 'Swim back! Swim back! to the other stream! In the morning the men will come here to barrel you!" She went on dreamily. "Perhaps the fish wouldn't believe me. The fairy would have to do something to make me different. Perhaps when I wanted to, I could shine all over. Then the fish would believe that I really knew.

" 'But we can't swim back,' they'd say.

" 'Then let yourselves go and let the current take you down to the end of the island!' "

Could you call a thing an island that was practically standing on end? It looked more like a cascade of rocks and willows. A real island ought to float, Alice thought, but then she came back with growing satisfaction to her story.

"When I explained, all bright and queer as I would be, the fish would let the water carry them down. Maybe there'd be a few deaf ones, but I'd go and shout to them and explain. Then when all the herring were safe on the right side, it would be morning and I'd turn into a little girl again, just before the men came. They'd be terribly surprised to see that there wasn't a single fish under the chute. They'd look and look, and ask questions, and I'd just sit there acting surprised, too, and I'd have my lieutenants among the fish stationed in the right places——"

"Now let's follow the path," said Alice's mother, not knowing she was interrupting Alice's thoughts, but before she left the intersection of the streams, Alice saw her flapping her coat in a queer way.

"What *are* you doing, Mother?" she asked, surprised.

Her mother, even in the moonlight, looked a little ashamed. "I was thinking I might be able to get some more of them to go the safe way," she admitted.

So grown people felt that way, too—at least grown ladies.

But Alice had already attended to all that. She scarcely noticed that the basin was as packed with fish as ever.

A little path led above the tumbling stream, now and then crossing it on rustic bridges. On one side were the willows and on the other the chicken yards and windows at the backs of houses, sometimes lighted, in oblongs of yellow which looked very lovely in the white moonlight. They were no longer alone. Two men and a woman were coming down the path toward them, and a large boy from the Mills whom Alice knew at school was standing at one of the small basins, watching the herring go up a ten-foot slide of white water.

When Alice spoke to him he looked up, but instantly looked down at the water again.

"Hello," he said, and then he pointed out to them all a fish with some of the scales rubbed off its side.

"I've been watching that fish more than an hour," he said, "and gosh, it hasn't made this stretch yet. Every time it tries it gets carried back into the basin again. It rests a while and then it tries again. It makes me tired just to watch it. Look! There it goes!"

Alice saw the marked fish dart upward into the white rush of the water. The stream was very shallow here and the herring, about a foot long, showed plainly, thrusting itself forward against the full onrush of the current. One foot, two feet, three feet upward it went and Alice held her breath.

The herring was going slower now, but still mounting. It seemed impossible that it could still be climbing. Then there was an awful moment when it hung in the stream unable to go forward, and in another second it was dashed downward into the basin, where the curve gave it some protection.

"A fish *couldn't* get up that!" Alice said angrily. It seemed to her that too much was being demanded of these poor herring. A person never had to work like that, no, not even with arithmetic. Yet as she spoke she saw a fish make the slide and reach the basin above. No one could tell how many times *that* one had tried as it wasn't wounded. She saw the marked one start off again. This time it came within six inches of the upper lip before it was carried back.

"Let's go on!" she said, tugging at her father's hand. "I can't bear to watch."

After that they saw only fish that looked all alike, some resting at the foot of cascades, some darting up them, a few succeeding and more failing. At the very top they stood watching an occasional fish make its way into the quiet water of the pond. The herring seemed bewildered by the sudden peace. They had fought so long to be here, and now that they *were* here, at last, they scarcely seemed to know what to do.

"It takes about twenty-four hours for a herring to go that

quarter of a mile," said Alice's mother. "I suppose some take longer."

Alice thought of the fish they had watched. On their way back, the boy was still standing on the bridge, dark against a bright strip of moonlight on the stream.

"Did it get up?" Alice asked.

"Yes, but there's another one I'm watching now," he said. Alice had no intention of giving her heart to another fish. *That* one was over the worst stretch, and was probably all right now. It was her fish and she needn't worry about it anymore. But as she walked down the path, her feet avoiding the stones all by themselves, she was aware of that dense, completely silent effort beside her.

"I wish they *stayed* in the sea!" she said explosively.

"So do I," said her mother.

"But it's beautiful and thrilling," said her father. "Think how—"

But Alice couldn't think about fish anymore. She lifted her face to the moon, and stared into its white, cold brightness. Then she heard a clock striking. One, two, three, four, five, six, seven, eight, nine, ten, eleven. It was eleven o'clock and here she was, up and dressed—yes, dressed in silver.

Now we begin to remember
(The herring say)
Ponds that lie in the valleys
Far away;

Waters where we were born
Fresh and sweet,
Where the shadows of green trees lie
Cool in the heat.

Sometimes a leaf falls down,
Or butterfly,
Then comes the mighty ice
Arching our sky.

Dear fitful changing ponds
—Not like this sea!—
How sweet your waters lie
In memory!

How sweet the little coves
Fragrant with fern—
Come! (all the herring cry)
Let us return!

A thousand miles to us
Nothing shall seem,
No fear shall turn us back
Swimming upstream!

For we once more recall
(The herring say)
Ponds among quiet hills
Far, far away.

XVI

LIVE HEIRLOOMS

A NEW family had moved into the gray-shingled house next door. There were Mr. and Mrs. Fairbanks and a two-year-old boy John. Alice's mother and father called on Mr. and Mrs. Fairbanks and said they were very nice indeed, and Alice tried to make John's acquaintance in his play pen on fine sunny mornings, but he was a difficult child to play with, because he always kept his back turned toward her no matter where she stood. He had two sieves and a dipper with a hole in it which he loved; he wanted to be left alone with them, and if Alice tried to attract his attention too much he would scream at the top of his lungs without changing his expression in the least. So Alice soon left him to himself and his tins, prepared to wait until John grew older.

But if John was a disappointment, the Fairbankses had other things to interest Alice. The first of these was Grandmother Jenkins' goose, which lived in a little house of her own, with a yard about it. Every afternoon she was allowed out to the small pond that lay back of the orchard, but at dusk she waddled home again to her own little pen.

She was a handsome creature, gray with black on her wingtips and a white breast and small wise-looking eyes. There was nothing old-looking about her, but Mrs. Fairbanks said that she was more than fifty years old and as a young goose had been given to Mrs. Fairbanks' own grandmother on her wedding day. She had been taken a hundred miles to her mistress' new home in Paris Hill, in a crate strapped to the back of a wagon, hissing all the way. Grandmother Jenkins had always valued her as the one living thing she had brought with her from Dresden, where she had been born, and Grandmother Jenkins' daughter and now her granddaughter had always taken the best of care of her because she was Grandmother Jenkins' goose.

172

After hearing this, Alice stared at the old goose with a new respect and Grandmother Jenkins' goose stared back at her with a proud expression, the look of one who has always had her wishes obeyed. Alice used to bring her watercress from the brook, which the goose liked very much, and after she had gobbled it down, she would turn and stare at Alice for a long time.

But if Grandmother Jenkins' goose was queen of the back-yard, Grandfather Thomas' parrot ruled the house. His cage hung in the dining-room window, in the sun. The first time that Alice noticed him happened to be on a warm morning when the windows were opened, and as she walked by the house she heard a hoarse voice singing:

> "*Ha-ha-ha,*
> *You and me,*
> *Little brown jug,*
> *I love thee!*"

Alice had never known a parrot at all well and she thought, "What a funny way for Mr. Fairbanks to be singing! And why isn't he at business?"

Then the voice went on and she had to stop to listen to it.

> "*If I had a cow*
> *That gave such milk,*
> *I'd dress her all*
> *In the finest silk!*"

And then came such a burst of laughter that Alice started to walk quickly away. But just then out of the tail of her eyes she saw something pink and gray moving, and again came the harsh loud laugh.

"Why, it's a parrot!" said Alice to herself. "I never saw a pink and gray one before."

So the next day when she brought watercress to Grandmother Jenkins' goose, and found Mrs. Fairbanks hanging up dishcloths near the pen, she asked her about the parrot.

"Come in and see him," said Mrs. Fairbanks. "He's a cross old bird, but we're very fond of him."

"Is he old, too?" asked Alice with wide eyes.

Mrs. Fairbanks gave her jolly laugh. "Some people have a great many antique chairs and beds, Alice," she said, "but the heirlooms we seem to have inherited in this family are birds. This is my husband's grandfather's parrot that he brought back from Africa on one of his voyages there. Polly, this is Alice, our neighbor. Alice, this is Grandfather Thomas' parrot. Now you've been introduced."

The parrot hung by one foot from his perch, and rapidly covered and uncovered his eyes with their lids. Most of the top of his head was bald, but Alice had never seen anything so bright and bold as his glance.

"Hello, hello, hello, hello," he said, feeling the bar with his thick pointed tongue.

"Hello, Polly," said Alice, staring back at him. "Are you older than Grandmother Jenkins' goose?"

The parrot who was climbing up the bars of his cage with the help of beak and claws did not answer, but Mrs. Fairbanks chuckled.

"My husband and I spend hours trying to make that out. It's a game with us," she said. "Grandfather Thomas was in command of the *Midas*, sailing out of Round Pond for the African Coast, from 1872 to 1885, but we don't know on which trip he brought back this parrot. We've looked up the logs, but he mentions monkeys and parrots in almost every one of them. And then we don't know if this was a young parrot or not when he got it. But Grandmother Jenkins' goose is a home body and we know all about her. She was born in 1873 and went to Paris Hill in 1874."

The parrot swung three times around his hanging perch and whistled derisively. Then he dropped to the long rod, sidled to the bars, and cocking his head said, "Pretty Polly, pretty Polly," in a coaxing voice.

"He's an awful beggar," said Mrs. Fairbanks, "but you may give him a lump of sugar, Alice. Look out for your fingers, though. He likes to nip when he can."

"That's very bad of you when people are giving you sugar," said Alice severely.

"He *is* a bad old thing," agreed Mrs. Fairbanks with an air of pride.

Alice liked Grandmother Jenkins' goose better than she did Grandfather Thomas' parrot, but she thought about them both a good deal. She decided to write about them for her term theme in English. It was easy to imagine about Grandmother Jenkins' goose, especially somehow now when the branches were hanging down with the young leaves looking like flowers, and the goose came walking through the growing grass, reaching out her long neck now and then to catch an insect. Alice could just imagine Grandmother Jenkins in a little bonnet with roses on it, and the creaking of the wheels, and the goose hissing crossly in her crate.

But it was harder to imagine Africa, and the low jungle coming down to the beach and black men paddling out in crude canoes, one of them carrying a pink and gray parrot. Mr. Fairbanks showed her the old logs of the *Midas* with drawings sometimes in the margins showing unusual sea birds or the outlines of harbors and islands as seen from the sea, called land-falls he told her. Every entry began with the wind: there might be fever on the ship, or even mutiny; the supplies might be running low, or one sailor might have stabbed another in a fight—but the wind always came first.

It gave Alice a rather excited feeling now to hear her

father say at breakfast, "Nice southwest wind this morning. I think it will clear by noon."

That's just what Captain Thomas would have said at breakfast before he began his day, she knew.

Besides the logs, Mr. Fairbanks showed Alice the other things he had which had come from Africa. First there was the god carved out of wood with a burned look around the legs where the Captain's wife, Mrs. Thomas, had once thrown it into the fire because it was heathen, and she didn't think it looked lucky; but she had pulled it out again because, after all, it was her husband who had brought it back from across the sea.

And then there was an elephant's tusk with carving on it, and a big wooden comb a foot high, very beautifully carved, too.

These things which she had actually handled Alice tried to bring into her theme. But she was dissatisfied. She couldn't catch all that strangeness in words. She couldn't make it seem all a part of that pink and gray bird joggling up and down in his cage and blinking his bright wicked-looking eye.

But she must have got part of it down, for Miss Dreer read her theme aloud to the whole school, and for several days children came to ask Mrs. Fairbanks if they might see the old goose and the parrot that came from Africa.

One day when Alice was sitting reading in her favorite

177

apple tree, she became aware that Grandmother Jenkins' goose was honking and honking. Mrs. Fairbanks had taken John in his carriage and gone somewhere. There was no one at their house.

Alice tried to go on reading, but the honking troubled her. "It can't be a fox," she said at last, climbing down from her perch angrily. "Do be still, you silly old thing, I'm coming."

Alice couldn't see anything wrong about the goose pen, but certainly the gray goose was disturbed. Her honking never stopped. Then Alice, looking about vaguely, saw the smoke coming out of the dining-room windows of the house. There was not a sound from the parrot.

"Perhaps he's dead," she thought as she began to run for the back door. Alice never remembered to be afraid when there was danger: it was perhaps part of her bad memory that she forgot about herself altogether at such times. Marcia would have been surprised to see how fast Alice could run when she wanted to, and how the door opened at her first touch.

Into the kitchen she tore; the pantry was full of smoke, but she ran through it. She saw flames along the floorboard on the far side of the dining room, but neither they nor the choking in her throat stopped her as she dragged a chair under the cage, pulled herself up onto it, and lifted the cage down. It was heavy. She was choking and coughing and couldn't run now, but she dragged the cage along with her, through the door, into the pantry, into the kitchen, and out of doors again. She still had it when she reached her own back door and gasped out to Olga that the Fairbanks' house was on fire.

Olga ran to the telephone and in a few minutes there was a banging of bells and the fire engine came up.

While the firemen were putting out the flame (which they did in the end with only the dining room burned from a cross-circuit in the old electric wiring behind the walls), Alice was watching the parrot who sat on the floor of his cage shivering violently, with his white wrinkled eyelids pulled down over his eyes.

"Don't die, Polly," said Alice softly. "It's all right now, don't die, please."

She had felt sick at her stomach herself, but now she was feeling better. But the parrot continued his awful silence. How hard it was going to be to tell Mr. and Mrs. Fairbanks that Grandfather Thomas' parrot had been killed after all, though she had done all she could to save him! A tear trickled down her face and fell off her chin. She reached for her handkerchief.

Just at that moment Alice felt a painful tweak of the other hand which still held the bars of Polly's cage. Jerking it away, she stared indignantly at Grandfather Thomas' par-

179

rot, which was suddenly looking very wide-awake and self-satisfied.

"You bad old thing!" Alice said angrily. "That's a nice way to act after I've just saved you!"

The parrot pulled himself back on his perch by his beak and began cleaning one claw, singing to himself off key:

"Ha ha ha,
You and me . . ."

"Ha ha ha,
You and me . . ."

"They didn't teach you any manners in Africa," said Alice severely. But she didn't mean it. She was like Mrs. Fairbanks, proud that Grandfather Thomas' parrot *was* a wicked old bird.

Then she went to get her book, which she had dropped by the goose pen when she first saw the smoke. The fire engine had gone; the last heavy voice was silenced. A robin was singing in a tree. Alice stood still for a moment feeling the accustomed peace. Grandmother Jenkins' goose looked at her for a while, and then went off stalking a butterfly that had lighted on the eaves of her little house. It might have been yesterday afternoon.

Alice took her book and climbed back into the crotch of her favorite apple tree.

Song of Grandfather Thomas' Parrot

Far off, far off
Those forests lie
Beneath a heavy
Molten sky

Where I was born—
Oh, never more
At dusk shall I hear
Lions roar,

Nor see the monkeys
Leap and sway
From branch to branch
At dawn of day!

Behold me now,
Across the sea,
Watching mild ladies
Pour out tea!